Dragon's Vow

Irish Honor, Volume 1

Amara Holt

Published by Amara Holt, 2024.

Dragons Vow

Prologue

Cillian

Past

The sky today has a smoky hue, announcing the approach of a storm, and it perfectly matches the occasion. It's as if someone had set the scene for the final act of a tragedy.

I watch from afar as the bodies of my soldier and his wife are buried.

Juno, their pre-teen daughter and the only survivor, sits upright with her hands clasped in her lap. Instead of watching as her parents' coffins are lowered into the ground, as one might expect, she twists something in her hands.

"Look at what she's holding," I order one of my men, because I don't want to approach the girl.

Although I intend to provide everything she will need now that she's an orphan, I will do so from a distance.

"Where are you going to send her?" Oisin, the man who acts as my secretary in the *Syndicate* and who is almost like a member of my family, asks.

"She has an aunt in Ireland."

"Look, I don't know shit about kids, but the girl has already lost her parents. Sending her to another country would strip her of any sense of security. *Family and home.*

"Maybe that's exactly what she needs: to forget the past."

"No one forgets what she's witnessed, Cillian. If you want my opinion, she's already damaged. Why make it worse by taking her out of her country?"

I don't disagree. Even though she's so young, it's impossible for her to ever forget the circumstances in which she lost her family. However, at least in Ireland, she'll be raised by someone of her own blood.

I see my man position himself behind her, probably to do what I asked.

"Juno can't stay here. I'll give her a new chance to start over, away from our world," I say.

"I doubt she'll make it. As I said before, at her age, she'll carry what happened with her forever, but I'll believe you know what you're doing. Now, let's get to the point: what about the son of a bitch who caused all this? What will we do with him?"

"We have no idea who he is, but I'm a patient man. He might hide, but I'll find him. When that happens, he'll wish he had never crossed paths with the Cavanagh family."

"It's a bracelet with a charm on it," my man informs when he returns. "A tiger, I think."

"Interesting, *Dragon*," Oisin says. "Could it be her Chinese zodiac sign? Because tiger and dragon are complementary signs. Maybe it was written from the start that their lives would be intertwined."

"I'm not superstitious. My mother was," I say, though I also believe in symbols. I wouldn't be Irish if I didn't take them seriously. "I've made up my mind. I'll send her to stay with her aunt in Dublin."

I start walking toward my car, surrounded by my soldiers.

"I did what I could," I try to convince myself, though inside, guilt eats away at me.

I have no doubt that if Juno ever learns the truth about my real involvement in her story, she'll hate me.

Chapter 1

Cillian

Boston

Ten Years Later

"It's done," my younger brother, Odhran, says as he enters my office. "Did the son of a bitch suffer?"

I waited too long for my revenge. Oliver Wilson hid for years, but only recently did I find out why: he was covered by the Albanian mafia. When I finally located the man I've been searching for a decade, I couldn't make him pay with my own hands because the bastard was sent to prison for attempting to kill Joaquín Oviedo's fiancée.

The idiot was stupid enough to try to hurt the woman of a prosecutor who, besides being incorruptible, seems like a bloodhound when he starts tracking a lead. However, Joaquín, always acting within the law, did what any good man would do: he made the miserable pay according to human justice.

I don't believe in it. In my world, I am the one who hands down the death sentence and carries it out. Like so many others who dared to cross my path, Oliver paid with his life.

He pulls a disposable phone from his pocket and hands it to me.

"What do you think? I instructed them not to make it quick. We did it the old-fashioned way: he was beaten with stones inside socks."

I take the phone and scroll through the five photos of what remains of the bastard.

"Yeah, I can't deny that they did a *hell of a job*."

In fact, I bet they'll take a while to identify the dead prisoner.

"Are you going to ask the prosecutor for a *favor*?"

"Probably not, but I'll let him know that I'm the one who rid the world of his enemy. Maybe he'll see it as a peace offering."

"From what you've shown so far, I doubt it. Just last year, he sent three of our men to prison. Joaquín is a bit like you, if you want my opinion. The difference is that they operate on opposite sides of the law."

I nod. If the man didn't do what he does, which is basically disrupt my business, I'd probably admire him.

"Joaquín Oviedo doesn't fool me. The only thing that sets us apart is that he works to punish the guilty with the backing of the law, and I do it my way. But I have no doubt that beneath his superhero facade, there's a savage capable of killing for his family."

"Who would have thought you'd execute a man because of a prosecutor!"

I remain silent long enough for him to understand.

It doesn't take long for my brother to shake his head back and forth.

"It wasn't because of him. You would have killed him anyway. What the hell did Oliver Wilson do to you?"

"Ten years ago, he seduced the wife of one of my men."

My brother didn't know the details of the mess involving Juno's family.

"How stupid. Messing with one of our women? But what's the big deal? The world is full of betrayals."

"This soldier was madly in love with his wife. He killed her and then committed suicide in front of their eleven-year-old daughter. When we arrived at the house, she was in shock. I made a promise that I would get the person responsible for making her an orphan. It was long overdue to fulfill it."

I see the recognition in his face.

"That little girl you're talking about is Juno? Is that why you sent her to Ireland?"

"Yes."

"I don't know if it's true, but Kellan mentioned to *aunt* Orla the other day that the girl's cousins said she wants to come back to the United States."

I run my hands over my face.

"I know. Juno has been asking me for that for years, but I needed to make sure Oliver was out of the way."

"Now there's no reason to keep her away."

"Why are you so interested in this matter?"

"I'm not. I just like to be prepared for changes. Over the years, I've seen you watch her from a distance. I never interfered, but it's no secret that you keep track of every step the girl takes. The way you behave towards her is completely unusual. If Juno moves to Boston, she'll be something of an Achilles' heel for you."

He's very close to the truth, although he has no idea of the extent of what he's talking about.

I don't usually have regrets about the shit I've lived and done. For that, I'd need to care about someone, and I can count on one hand those who matter in my life. However, in the case of Juno and her family, the feeling of guilt is something I can't shake off.

"Your relationship with her is very strange, Cillian. Now, knowing Juno's true identity and that messed-up story with Oliver, may the devil keep him in hell, I understand you tried to avenge her family, but I don't get why you took on the task of keeping her protected all these years."

"I had my reasons," I say vaguely, not wanting to go down that path. "Now, let's focus on what matters: have the tracks about the money from our recent deals been erased?"

In our main business, money laundering, it's crucial to make the trail left in the process disappear. We provide *services* to billionaires and authorities around the world who can't justify, within the terms of the law, the fortune they possess. Most of the time, amassed through bribery.

"Everything is under control. The money has been sent to an offshore account in Central America and from there, it will be exchanged for virtual currencies for about a month. After that, no one will be able to trace its origin."

"We have to be extra careful. Joaquín Oviedo would love to know that we're taking about fifty million dollars out of the country to legitimize it for Senator Barlowe.

"That damn prosecutor is like a fucking hunter."

I shrug.

"I don't take it personally. Oviedo is doing his job just as we are doing ours. Just don't leave any traces and we'll be fine."

He continues talking about the Russians being in a war with Mexicans, but I'm no longer paying attention. Everyone should mind their own shit. To my misfortune, my cousin, who is also one of my trusted men, Lorcan, is the grandson of the *former Pakhan* Ruslan Vassiliev. The old man, whom I secretly admire, has this fucked-up idea of family, although Yerik, the current *Pakhan* Russian, and I don't want any agreements about our businesses.

I slide the pen I got for my birthday from *aunt* Orla—my father's sister-in-law, who raised us after they died—between my fingers. It's kind of a *tick* I have when my mind escapes to some secret place. When I can't keep the past where it should be.

Remorse is a fucked-up feeling. You can't get rid of it, no matter how hard you try, but taking care of Juno's safety in Ireland gives me the sense of at least easing my debt to Satan, in this shithole that is my life.

Odhran says his goodbyes, and my hand goes to the phone.

I know I shouldn't because the less contact I have with her, the better, but I also know I'll do it anyway. Making sure she's safe is like a fucking compulsion. I check on her by phone at least every two months since I sent her to Ireland. Even though there are people watching her closely since then, I like to hear her tell me she's fine.

The phone rings only three times before I hear her voice, and I wonder if she does it on purpose. Juno always answers on the third ring.

Yes, I'm a control freak who doesn't miss a single detail.

Despite that, I'm always very straightforward when I want to check on her well-being, never taking longer than necessary or letting her ask questions.

"Juno."

"Mr. Cillian? I didn't expect you to call today."

I can feel her vibration even from a distance, as if magnetic waves keep us connected. I haven't seen her since she was a little girl, although I can tell, from our phone interactions, that the girl is fucking restless.

"I mean, I'm glad you called, I just wasn't expecting it," she corrects, nervously, perhaps afraid of offending me.

In a twisted way, these conversations with Juno keep me connected to my human side. It's like a sinner approaching purity, though never allowing himself to look too closely.

"I heard you want to come back to the United States, Juno. I will allow it, as long as you're willing to obey my rules."

Chapter 2

Juno

I feel like slapping myself for the way my heart races just hearing the voice of my protector, Cillian O'Callaghan.

I've gotten used to these phone calls since I moved to Ireland, but lately, I've been anticipating them anxiously, even though there's no reason for it. He always asks me the same questions, as if he's following a script. When I was younger, he wanted to know how I was doing in school, if I was eating properly, or if I needed anything. Now that I'm older, he asks about my culinary school, which I'm almost done with.

The strange thing is that he's never really been present in my life, so I didn't understand why he cared so much.

Of course, it was Cillian and his men who found me alone at home the day my parents died, and I understand he might feel responsible in some way since Dad worked for him, but after ten years, I thought he'd stop caring. Yet, he still checks in on me, calling almost religiously.

These aren't warm phone calls or the kind a relative would make. They're more like something a school principal would do, a sort of obligation.

Since my father belonged to the *Syndicate*, I don't think I'll ever be completely free. His former associates will always be around.

Even though I was a pre-teen when they died, I knew my father was involved in something illegal. In fact, all my friends at the time were children of *Syndicate* members. That was always my world.

"I heard you want to return to the United States, Juno. I'll allow it, as long as you're willing to obey my rules."

I repeat what he just said, unsure if I heard correctly. Since I turned eighteen, I've been asking Mr. Cillian to let me move to the United States, and the answer has always been the same: *not yet.*

I accepted his refusal because I learned to respect him as *Dad* did. Besides, even over the phone, he's not someone you'd want to argue with. I grew up hearing his name at home—both my parents' home and the one I live in now with relatives—as the late husband of my aunt also belonged to the *Syndicate*, and she and my cousins speak of the *Boss* with reverence.

"Why now?" I ask, before I can stop myself.

Two seconds later, I regret the stupid question.

"Don't want to go anymore? I thought it was your greatest desire."

It might be my madness, but I'm almost sure he expects me not to actually go. Until now, he's only given me "no" answers without explaining why, so, terrified he might back out, I quickly add:

"That's not what I meant. Of course I want to go back. When can I leave?"

"First, we need to talk about the rules. Nothing will change when you get here. There will still be someone taking care of you, and you can never go out without a phone. I'll also need to know who you're making friends with."

I roll my eyes, irritated, but knowing I'm not holding the best cards at the moment. In Ireland or in the United States, I'll remain under his control.

"Yes, sir," I reply, almost biting my tongue. "Are those the only rules?"

"Those are the main ones, but there are others. I want you to continue studying until you graduate. I know it's almost time. I heard you dream of opening your own business, and I'll make sure that happens. Otherwise, keep being a good girl and we won't have any problems."

And if I don't, what will you do? I really want to ask, but I'm not crazy.

I know Cillian is not someone you challenge. He is feared by both allies and enemies.

"I'm not a rebel, sir. I intend to live my life, but I don't want to be a headache. I've never even considered stopping my studies. And yes, I really want to open my bakery, but I don't want any favors."

"Did I imply that you had a choice, Juno? Because if I did, it was a mistake. You will return to the United States, but you will never stop being part of our family. I thought you already knew that. Everything I think necessary to ensure you have a good life, I will do. There's no room for your questioning."

I shiver at the cold tone but try to stay calm. I want to return so badly and I'm not going to screw it up now.

"Where will I live?" I ask, pretending sweetness so he doesn't notice my agitation.

"I'll arrange everything."

"And what about work? You should know, sir, that I have a part-time job at a café here in Dublin. Until I finish college, since there's only one semester left, I don't want to be doing nothing. Can't I work in the fights?"

"How do you know about that?"

Oh my God! Me and my big mouth.

"I... um... I heard my cousins talking about some girls performing in the fights organized by the *Syndicate*. It could be something to keep me occupied until I finish my studies."

He stays silent for so long that I'm afraid he's hung up, and I almost faint with relief when he says:

"I'll think about it. For now, start organizing your move here. When everything is in order, get in touch. Tomorrow, housing and your enrollment in a college here in Boston will be arranged. Someone will contact you to get the details for the registration."

"How will I call you to let you know I'm ready to go? It's always you who calls me."

"I'll make sure my private number reaches you. It's not the one we're using now. You should always call me on the other one."

"Alright, but I'm sure I won't need much time. I mean, there's still a month before the next semester starts, so it's more than enough to get my things together. As long as my enrollment at the university is done, I think everything will be fine."

"Next week, then?"

"Already?" I almost shout with joy, but then I remember who I'm speaking to and correct myself: "Yes, next week is perfect, sir!"

He hangs up without saying goodbye, and I'm not surprised, as it's not the first time. If there's one thing I've learned about my protector through these phone calls over the years, it's that he's not a soft man.

I run to the kitchen, where my aunt is finishing preparing our dinner.

"He's letting me go back!" I yell, jumping around like a madwoman.

She doesn't show the same enthusiasm. After placing the shepherd's pie in the oven, she turns to me.

"Are you sure about this, Juno?"

"Aunt, you know it's my greatest wish to go back home."

"Here is your home."

"I know," I say, embarrassed. "But the United States is home too. I can barely remember my life there. The last memory..." I start but stop, as I don't like to dwell on the past.

"I know, dear. I didn't mean to make you sad, and that's exactly why I think you should think about whether you really want to go back. What's there to remember fondly? From what you've told me, not much."

"I'll be fine. Mr. Cillian said he'll help me find a job, and I'll finish college."

"I don't like the idea of you going back to that world. Here, you're protected by us."

"Your husband was part of the *Syndicate*, and so are your children. In fact, I never left *that world*, as you call it," I say, but then I regret it, because I adore her and don't want to argue. "My father was Cillian's trusted soldier, Aunt. I'm sure that's why he's taken care of me until now and will continue to do so forever, I think. Until the tragedy happened, they were my family too." I approach and hug her. "It's not like I'm going to the death row. If things don't work out, I can always come back, right?"

"You know that's true. My home will always be open to you, Juno."

"He said I could move in a week."

"So soon? Why the rush?"

"I need to get my life in order before starting the final semester and also find a job."

She starts setting the table, and I go to the cupboard to get glasses.

"Are we alone today?"

"No, the boys are already on their way," she says, referring to my cousins. "Juno, you know you're not going to live the American dream as just any girl, right? The people you'll be around, just like my children and their father, my dear Fionn, are not the good guys."

"And yet, you loved your husband with all your soul."

"Yes, I loved him. I still love him, even after so many years since he passed away. We don't choose who we fall in love with. When the heart decides, all we can do is accept it."

I finish setting the table and turn back to face her.

"I'll be fine. I promise. From my limited life experience, there are no good guys, Aunt. Even with our parents, we're not safe."

She gives me a sad smile because we both know what I'm talking about.

"Do you think Mr. Cillian knows the whole truth about what happened at your house the day your parents died?"

"No. I don't think so. And what does it matter? It's the past."

"Not inside you."

"Not yet, but one day it will be. In a few years, I'll have my own family, and it will be perfect like yours. And then, what I lived through in the few years I had with my parents will just be a bad memory."

Chapter 3

Juno

Boston — Massachusetts

Two Weeks Later

I was so grateful to be able to return to the United States that, at first, I didn't expect much more than the right to be here, but certainly, I didn't anticipate what actually happened.

Fifteen days ago, I set foot on American soil, and so far, I've only had two exchanges of messages with Mr. Cillian.

He sent women to help me organize my apartment — I'll never confess this to anyone, but I feel like I'm in a dream, finally living as an adult — and to stock it with whatever I need. They also went with me to the college to sort out the bureaucratic issues of the transfer, since I'll have to take three courses that weren't part of my student curriculum in Dublin.

I was grateful, but I don't want this kind of service anymore. I am perfectly capable of taking care of my home and my life on my own.

As for the bodyguards he put in charge of me, there's nothing to be done for now, but I think as time passes and Cillian sees that I'm a grown-up girl, I'll be able to live my life normally.

Who can stand being watched forever?

"The Syndicate members," a voice in my head immediately responds.

Yeah, but I'm not a member and don't have any connection to them other than Mr. Cillian's protection, so probably, in a few months, I'll be completely free.

I've heard many stories about how protective they are of the widows and orphans of their men, but with me, I think they're overdoing it. I can't step outside the building without someone following me.

They don't speak or show any friendliness, but they remain like my shadow. And my outings haven't been spectacular. I took a walk to get to know Boston again, because besides the fact that I was very young when I left, even then I didn't go much beyond our neighborhood.

We didn't do normal family activities because of my father's *profession*.

No, to be honest, it wasn't just because of that, but also because my mother never seemed happy with us.

I push her thoughts away, as I have done since that night. I don't feel guilty for not missing her because the truth is, I never forgave her. I do make sure to remember my father every night, and I won't go to bed without asking God to have mercy on his soul for what he did.

I look around the apartment, sighing, a little tired of doing nothing. My return home has been a fiasco. I need to take action. I didn't come to Boston to be locked up like a bird in a gilded cage.

Enough with the messages. I'm going to call Cillian.

When I arrived in the United States, I was given a phone with the recommendation to discard the old one. I don't even know why I need one, since I have no one to call except Aunt Eimear, who has been talking to me every day via video call.

I walk over to the bedside table to get the phone, but before I can reach it, the doorbell rings.

The security guards wouldn't have let just anyone up, so it must be... Could it be?

My heart races at the prospect of meeting in person, for the second time, the one who has been my protector from afar. I remember very little of his face, and Aunt Eimear only had a single photo of him when he was younger. The *Syndicate* members don't expose themselves on social media or allow themselves to be photographed. I know this because even in our home, Dad didn't like us keeping records of the three of us, and that's one of the reasons I have so few memories of my childhood.

Forgetting the bodyguards' recommendations, I open the door without checking the peephole first.

To my disappointment, it takes me two seconds to realize that the man standing in front of me isn't my protector, though he does resemble Cillian.

"Are you out of your mind?"

I am so shocked by the aggressive tone of his voice that I take a step back as he enters the apartment.

"Answer me."

"I..."

"Don't you have any rules to follow, girl? What the hell was that, opening the door without checking who it was? I could be a rapist."

I feel all the blood drain from my body.

"Are you?"

"Sweetheart, if I were, you'd be lost by now. Welcome to Boston, Juno."

I don't even have time to respond, and he's already looking around the apartment.

"I came to check, at my brother's request, if you're settled in well."

"Brother?"

"Cillian."

"My protector," I say, without thinking.

A corner of his mouth lifts in a vague imitation of a smile.

"He was never labeled that, but I think, in your case, it works well."

"Sorry if I sound idiotic," I say, closing the door, because if he's Cillian's brother, I don't believe he means me any harm, "but who are you?"

"Odhran O'Callaghan."

Wow, now I understand why he looked like he was about to fly at my neck when I opened the door without checking who it was. In theory, I know everything about Cillian, and this is his younger brother, who my cousins said is known within the *Syndicate* as the *Mad Lion*.

The nickname seems quite fitting, both because his dark, thick hair is in urgent need of a cut, and because of his volatile temperament.

He doesn't make any move to greet me. Instead, he sits in an armchair as if he owns *my* apartment.

Yes, I know it's borrowed, but it's the first time I have a place to call my own, even if it's temporary, and I feel possessive about the place.

"Nice to meet you... I guess." I sit in the farthest armchair and even though I don't look at him, I can see he follows my movements like a feline watching its prey. "You said Mr. Cillian asked you to check on me. Why didn't he do it himself?"

The man looks at me for so long that I start to feel uneasy. I have no idea what he's thinking because his expression is blank, but I'm not sure if it's a good thing. I mean, he doesn't scare me... not much, at least. It's not like I think he'll attack me at any moment, because besides being who he is, I have good instincts. I grew up with four cousins who taught me how to defend myself when necessary. I think the unease I feel is because the man in front of me is inscrutable.

"My brother doesn't have time for this."

I pretend that doesn't affect me, but it hurts, because it was exactly what I thought: that despite having let me come and somehow feeling responsible for me, I'm not important enough for him to check on me personally.

"And you do?" I ask recklessly. His calm is irritating me.

"Not really, but I heard you want to work in the fights. Is that serious?"

His eyes roam over my body and for the first time, I feel a pang of apprehension. He's evaluating me like a man would. However, it lasts only a few seconds. Then, the indifferent expression returns.

"Yes, it is," I reply quickly, not wanting to miss the opportunity. "I'll start studying in a few weeks, but from what I've heard, the fights are at night, right?"

"Uh-huh. Have you ever watched UFC?"

"I have. My cousins love it, and one of them works for the 'competition.'"

"So you'd be like those girls holding the signs. You'll be dressed very little, sweetheart. Is that okay with you?"

In some way, I feel like he's testing me.

"Totally. I can handle it," I lie, because the closest I've ever come to wearing something short was at the pool, with a very modest swimsuit.

He stands up, still showing no sign of what he's thinking, and begins to walk toward the door.

"I'll send someone to pick you up on Saturday. The fights start at nine. Be ready by six because the girls will train you so you know what to do."

"Will Mr. Cillian be okay with this? With me working in the fights?"

"Why would he care?" he says, leaving and closing the door behind him.

Yeah, why would he care? I'm nothing to him.

Fear and excitement play inside me.

It's the first time since my father died that I'll really get close to the *Syndicate*. Even if for a short time, I'll get to know a bit of this world.

Chapter 4

Juno

Since Odhran left on Wednesday, I haven't received any messages from my protector, but since *Mad Lion* said he came to check on me at Cillian's request, I assume he knows I'll be working the fights.

As agreed, at six o'clock sharp, one of the security guards came to tell me to come downstairs. I'm incredibly nervous but also very excited. I'm going to earn my own money and start saving to become independent, and maybe even, in the future, move to another state.

The man who brought me to my first job on American soil parks in what seems to be an abandoned building, as if no one lived there. However, I know from my cousins that, contrary to what Cillian's brother said, the only similarity between the *Syndicate* fights and the UFC is the reasonable amount of sweat and blood involved, because the Association organizing these fights here is clandestine.

I feign confidence as I get out of the vehicle and also pretend not to notice the men's stares. If I'm going to wear as little as the girls who work the televised fights, shyness won't do me any good.

I understand how things work in this environment because even though my time with Dad, an active member of the *Syndicate*, was short, I grew up with my cousins, all soldiers in Cillian's organization on Irish soil.

I've lived in a bubble until now, but a mafia bubble, not a regular girl's. I know, for example, that I shouldn't give any confidence to the members, as they are womanizers, and even simple eye contact can cause complications.

Thus, as I enter the shabby-looking building, I keep my head high but focused straight ahead.

Playing indifferent isn't easy for me because I like people and usually talk a lot per minute, but in this strange environment, surrounded by guys looking at me like I'm a juicy steak, pretending to be an idiot might be a great tactic.

The place is already quite crowded, even with three hours to go before the fights start.

I have no idea where I'm supposed to go since the two men beside me don't say a word, just following me as if *I* should lead them.

Before I can open my mouth to ask whom I should speak to for directions on what to do, Odhran appears.

Okay, he might not be the friendliest guy in the world, but at this moment, I feel like we're childhood friends.

"Hi," I say, walking towards him, aware that several people have stopped talking to look at us.

"You're late."

I count to ten in my head, trying to calm down, because the man is too rude. I give up when I reach five. If I have to pretend to be something I'm not for the time I work here, I'm going to explode.

"You know full well it wasn't my fault. I didn't drive here; I came with the men you sent to pick me up."

"Don't mind him, sweetheart. It's not personal. He acts like an ass with everyone," someone says behind me, and when I turn to see who it is, I catch an older version of Odhran checking out my backside.

The man doesn't even try to hide it.

Jesus!

"He doesn't have a name, but I do," I say, annoyed.

"What?"

"He should introduce himself to me, not my ass."

To my surprise, several guys around us laugh, but I didn't say that jokingly. If these idiots think that just because I'm going to work the fights they can objectify me, they're very mistaken.

"I'm Kellan, sweetheart. Cillian's middle brother." He finally looks at me, and the first thing I notice is that the blue eyes are a familiar trait. All three O'Callaghan brothers have them.

"Nice to meet you. I'm..."

"I know, pretty ass," he says, but now I think he's just teasing me. "You're my brother's protégée, Juno Cavanagh. I was about to leave, but I changed my mind. I can't wait to witness his reunion with his 'little girl,'" he says, emphasizing that last word with irony.

"He... huh... is he coming?"

"Yes. He always makes at least one appearance at the fights. Now, if I were you, I'd hurry to get changed. Maria isn't in a good mood today."

"Who is Maria?"

"The woman who handles your... *uniform*," Odhran replies. "Take her to the locker room." He directs the security guards, and without another word, the two O'Callaghan family members leave me alone.

Fifteen minutes later, I need a lot of self-control not to say what I'm thinking as I hold the black corset, stockings, garter belt, and *high heels* in my hands.

This doesn't look like a fight uniform. Nothing like what I saw the girls on TV wearing; it's much more suited for a *strip club*.

"Can you walk in those heels?" the woman named Maria asks. Actually, she shouts as if I have trouble hearing.

"There are high heels in Ireland," I respond sweetly, but letting the venom drip from each word.

What does she think I am? A savage?

"Besides, I'm half American. I know more or less how civilized people dress."

She glares at me, and I'm sure she catches the irony, but she steps away without saying anything.

I sigh, with no desire to change, but I'm not a quitter, so even though I'm disheartened, I head for one of the dressing room booths because the idea of being naked in front of other women doesn't appeal to me.

Then I remember that I'm going to be nearly naked in front of a crowd, and for the first time, I wonder if I rushed into accepting this job.

"Don't mind her, dear. She always seems to be wearing her underwear inside out," a beautiful brunette says beside me. "I'm Elaine, by the way."

"Hi, my name is Juno, and I'm not upset with her bad mood, but with this outfit," I say, showing the clothes I'm holding.

"Oh, you're a newbie, huh? I thought you were transferred."

"Transferred?"

"Yes, there are places like this all over the country where... huh... the *Syndicate* operates."

Her voice drops lower as she finishes speaking, as if she's afraid of saying something she shouldn't.

"I have to go," she says, grabbing her own clothes. "Watch out for tripping when you enter the ring, Juno." She starts to walk away but then turns back. "And don't mind the whistles or rude comments you'll surely hear. They won't touch you unless you let them."

"I have no intention of letting them."

She shrugs and smiles.

"You never know. There are some pretty hot members, especially the boss and his relatives."

"You think... um... Cillian is attractive?" I ask, curious.

"Never seen him?"

"Not in person," I reply, without going into detail that the only time we faced each other was a decade ago, on what became the worst day of my life. Besides that, only the photograph from when he was much younger.

"Attractive"? No, he's scandalously good-looking, but if you want advice, stay away. If you have to choose one of the elite members, go for the two younger brothers, or even their cousin, Lorcan. They're womanizers, but much less intimidating than the *Boss*.

"No, you misunderstood... I..."

"I have to go, Juno. Good luck. See you around," she says, leaving me alone to process that information.

Not the part about Cillian being good-looking, of course. I already sensed that from the photo I saw and from meeting the two O'Callaghan family specimens... But from her saying the younger ones were less intimidating.

I know Cillian is a dangerous man. I've heard my cousins say that no one holds such a prominent position as the head of the Irish mafia without being respected and feared in equal measure. However, what confused me was that hearing that didn't scare me. It excited me.

Chapter 5

Cillian

There's a specific reason I'm here. I usually come to the fights in Boston, even if just briefly, but I don't usually stay long. However, I came tonight because my curiosity got the better of me.

I know Juno will be working, and even though I don't want to be close to her, something my brother said when he went to check on her intrigued me: that the girl would quickly become the attraction of the night's fights.

As far as I remember, there was nothing special about the girl. Thin, average height, hair the color of sand, blue eyes. Very much like her mother, Doireann, except for the hair color, as my friend's hair was brown.

She's the reason I protect Juno, not because of her father, my ex-soldier Grady, as everyone thinks. She was the only friend I had in Dublin. The one who stood by me during one of the worst moments of my life and who created memories that stay with me to this day.

The woman I failed.

I get out of the car and avoid people trying to talk to me. Few have the courage to approach because they know I don't waste words.

The place is packed, and the awareness that seems to work only in relation to Doireann's girl makes me question if it was a mistake to allow her to work the fights.

Not that I'm afraid something will happen to her. Those who don't know will soon find out that Juno is under my protection, which will shield her from any advances. My concern comes from having kept her all these years in a glass bubble, in Ireland, with her aunt and, mainly, with her cousins watching over her for me, along with the men who made sure no asshole got too close with ulterior motives.

Now she's starting her adult life in a country she barely knows.

But isn't it time for a reality check?

Juno will never be able to completely distance herself from our world because I won't allow it. I will protect her until my last breath on Earth, since I couldn't do so with her mother, but even I know that I can't keep her without exposing her to the real world — the ugly as hell one that would have been hers if her father hadn't changed the course of their lives.

My security team clears a path through the crowd. When I enter the area reserved for me, almost at the edge of the ring, the lights are already out.

I know the stakes are high tonight because Lorcan is fighting. He does it for fun or maybe because he's completely insane, but it's never been for money.

In daily life, my cousin is cold, and those who don't know him well might mistake him for a nice guy, but I've kept him with me his whole life, except for the time Grandpa wanted him to do his rite of passage by infiltrating the FBI, and I know his essence is exactly like mine and my brothers': we don't fear death, we challenge it every day.

The first fighter has been announced, and heavy rock music starts playing, which instantly gets my blood pumping as well.

Even though the *Syndicate* is involved in much more profitable businesses than the fights, I enjoy this atmosphere. It reminds me of my teenage years in Dublin, when I'd get into any fight for a few bucks.

I barely pay attention to the fight, but to those around me. There are some politicians and company directors with whom I *work*, disguised in caps and hoodies. They're not afraid to mix because they know they're not only on my payroll but under my protection as long as they do what I want.

I guess that being here, sure that it's an underground business, is their idea of danger.

None of them know what real danger is.

"She's one hell of a firecracker," Kellan says, sitting down next to me. "She's half-Irish, right?"

"Who?" I deflect.

"Your hot little protégée. The girl's got balls. In two minutes of conversation, she put me in my place. It's a shame I can't take a spin on that amusement park."

For the first time since he took the seat next to me, I look at him. I don't need to speak for him to understand.

"Fuck, what a bad mood. You know I don't go for the *saints*, but good luck trying to keep the guys off your girl. She's a sight to behold. Angelic face, killer body, and, for me, the highlight: a sharp tongue."

The fight ends, and after the announcement of the winner, the girls start to enter the ring. As always, the guys go wild.

I'm focused, however, on the reason I came here.

"Damn, that's what I call making an entrance," my brother mocks, and when I look at him, he's pointing to the screen where the camera follows the walk of a curvaceous blonde dressed in the typical girl uniform.

The men cheer and whistle, but no one dares to touch her, just as they don't with the other girls.

I know immediately that it's her.

I try to avert my eyes from her body because it feels fucking wrong to lust after her like everyone else is, but I can't help it. Her waist is impossibly slim — I think I could close it with my hands — and it tapers into long, thick thighs. Her breasts are almost spilling out of the black corset, and when she climbs the steps to enter the ring, I no longer need the screen to see the roundest, most perfect ass on the planet.

"So, happy to be reunited with your *little girl*?"

I don't answer, simply because I don't have a response to give.

"If you want my opinion, she's going to be a handful."

"She won't be. Juno is a good girl."

"Sorry to break it to you, but she's not a *girl*, brother. She's a delicious woman and I don't think she should stay here."

"No one will touch her knowing she's mine."

"That's the problem. She's not your woman, she's a protégée. Odhran mentioned something about her studying to be a pastry chef. Open a damn shop for her to sell what she bakes. Problem solved."

I think about what he's saying and try to analyze, if I listen to him, whether it's because I agree that Juno doesn't belong in the fighting world, or because it bothers me to see her nearly spilling out of that corset, knowing that most of the attendees are thinking about taking her to bed.

I don't know the real reason.

"She doesn't belong in this world, Cillian. I wanted you to see for yourself, but you've been in this too long to know that soon someone will go after her. Don't get me wrong. She seems to know how to defend herself, but as your protégée, she's a weak point for us."

He's right. When Odhran said something similar before Juno came, I thought it was just a bunch of bullshit mixed with his paranoia, but now I have to agree that keeping her close to the rings could end badly.

"I'll handle it."

"You were caught off guard too, weren't you? Didn't you look at photos of her over the years?"

"I never asked for any. Why would I? I talked to her occasionally on the phone, checked if she was okay. That was enough for me."

"If you had done that, you wouldn't be dealing with this problem now."

I look at her, still standing in the ring. Her chin is lifted as she parades with the sign announcing the next fight, but she looks uncomfortable.

She's pretending to be confident, but I didn't get to where I am without recognizing a liar.

Kellan is right, she doesn't belong in the rings.

Suddenly, she turns to where I am and our eyes meet. She stops walking and seems to forget what she was doing until the lights start to dim and she's called to leave.

I get up with the intention of going to find her and take her out of here.

My bodyguards start clearing a path, but before I can reach the exit, Odhran appears in front of me.

"I need to talk to you for two minutes."

"Not now."

"It's urgent. About one of the money shipments we discussed this morning."

Chapter 6

Juno

I should be working as an actress, not a pastry chef, which is what I plan to be in the future.

As I walked around the ring with the sign, a smile more fake than a three-dollar bill plastered on my face, as if being nearly naked in front of a crowd of men was nothing, I thought I was putting on an excellent performance.

Maybe I was, because I managed to ignore most of the obscene words and phrases I heard and almost congratulated myself for not letting it affect me, until my eyes met *his*.

From that point on, there was no way to pretend anything.

I knew he'd come, but now I realize I wasn't prepared to see him.

Amidst the shouting and all that testosterone, Cillian reigned, analytical and cold, among the rest of the mortals. I tried to look away from his eyes, but I couldn't.

He seemed to have the power to guess that I was playing a part. As if he knew I wasn't comfortable in this place and agreed that I didn't belong in this part of his world.

I was almost at the edge of the ring with his brother, Kellan, by his side, but even if the younger O'Callaghan wasn't there, I would have known it was him. I would never forget those eyes. I first saw them when I was still a girl.

They are deep eyes that say: I'm seeing through you.

As if he could recognize the unhappy girl I once was.

Could he? Most people think that losing my parents the way I did was a nightmare, but what they don't realize is that my nightmare began long before that.

Suddenly, the memory of that horrible night comes back—the final part, I mean. The moment when my protector came to get me, when he saved me.

I smothered it for a long time, but now, as I leave the ring, I remember when he looked at me and said the words: "I'll take care of you."

Cillian has no idea that at that moment, when everyone thought I was mourning my parents' deaths, I felt free.

It's a feeling of guilt and shame that I will carry for the rest of my life, but even though I will forever lament losing Daddy, I can't help but think that *she* got what she deserved.

I barely notice that I'm almost reaching the locker room, although I can vaguely hear the same obscenities being shouted by the male audience. When I arrive at the place where we change, I sigh with relief to see it's empty.

I can't leave yet. The night has barely begun, but at least I can be alone for a little while.

It doesn't last long. Seconds later, the door opens and an older man, around fifty, walks in.

It's not his appearance that makes me take a step back—he's just an average middle-aged man, and if I had to guess, wealthy—but the fact that he closes the door behind him.

"Unauthorized entry is prohibited."

Yes, I tend to say rehearsed lines when I'm nervous. I'm the queen of canned phrases.

When I worked at the café in Dublin and got really pissed off by an unfair customer complaint, instead of throwing coffee at the unlucky bastard, I would say something like: *the customer is always right.* In this case, specifically, I want the customer to go to hell, because no one needs to be a genius to know what this man is after.

"Not to me," he says and takes a step closer.

The urge to look back to see where I could run is almost uncontrollable. It wouldn't be the first time I had to flee from a man, but I'm no longer a scared and defenseless girl, I'm a woman. If he tries to touch me, he'll have to kill me first.

"To anyone. I don't know who you are and I don't care, but I'm not a prostitute. I'm working."

He looks me up and down, and it's more offensive than if he had insulted me.

"I don't know what kind of woman you're used to dealing with, sir, but I'll repeat once more: I'm not a prostitute. Now, get out."

"Speak to me in that tone again and you'll regret it, bitch."

I clench my fists by my sides, ready to defend myself.

Where the hell is everyone? Why isn't any of the other girls or even Maria coming in?

I decide to hell with caution.

"You can't touch me. I'm Cillian's protégée."

He throws his head back and laughs. Actually, he guffaws.

"Cillian is a businessman like me. He wouldn't make trouble with me over a little whore."

I don't believe that for a second. He wouldn't protect me for a lifetime just to let this bastard touch me by force.

With no pretense of maintaining dignity, the only thing that goes through my mind is that I'm going to die fighting. I take off my heels and hold them like a weapon, pointing them at him. His laughter grows and he advances toward me.

Terrified, when he gets too close, I hit him with the heel, striking his neck, but he still grabs my arm tightly.

A loud thud is heard and then Elaine appears, still dressed like me, in her *fight uniform*.

She doesn't ask anything, but literally flies onto the guy's back, wrapping her arms around his neck as if trying to choke him.

I take the chance to knee him in the groin, but even though he's almost doubled over in pain with Elaine on his back, his hand remains like a claw gripping my arm.

Adrenaline rushes through my body and I hit him with my shoe in every spot I can. He finally lets go of me, but then the back of his hand hits my face and everything turns to darkness.

I DON'T KNOW HOW MUCH time passes, but I hear distant shouting and my head hurts a lot. I force myself to open my eyes and when I manage to, the first person I see is the man who, while seeming so familiar, doesn't really know me.

"Mr. Cillian."

He doesn't speak, but I know he's holding something cold near my mouth. I pass my tongue over it and taste blood. I squeeze my eyes shut because the inside of my cheek is burning.

"What the hell happened here?" I hear *Mad Lion*'s voice, and then I see his face behind his brother. "Who did this to her?"

Nothing. Cillian just continues holding the ice pack against my face and looking at me in silence.

"What happened, Juno?" he finally asks, like so many times on the phone when he wanted to know if I needed anything.

"That man followed me," I say, wincing in pain. "I told him to leave, but he attacked me. Elaine tried to defend me, but... I think he managed to hit me."

I hate feeling vulnerable. I promised that no one would hurt me after my mother was gone, and now I'm here, in front of these two men, practically strangers, letting them see my weakness.

"Stay with her until I get back," he says to his brother. "Don't let anyone in except MacAlley, to examine her."

He leaves without looking at me again, but Odhran takes his place.

"I'm sorry about this, sweetheart," he says, tucking a strand of my hair behind my ear, in a completely different way than he had been treating me until now.

It's tempting to accept comfort from these dangerous and protective men too, but I don't want to show weakness.

"It wasn't that serious."

"Bullshit it wasn't, but you can be sure it won't happen again."

"I don't need promises."

"I don't think you understand *where* or *who* you're with, Juno. My brother considers you his protégée, which makes you "*ours*" to take care of. It's not your choice."

Chapter 7

Cillian

I'm not in a hurry as I walk to the basement. In fact, I slow my pace, trying to calm myself, because if I go in there feeling like this, it'll be a bloodbath, and this isn't the place to play like that.

I'm a fucking block of ice ninety-nine percent of the time, until someone invades my territory, and the undead asshole waiting for me crossed every line when he hit her.

I didn't spend a decade protecting the girl just for some son of a bitch to beat her up.

The image of Juno's swollen cheek comes to mind and the hatred I usually keep under control surfaces.

It's really a shame I don't have time to make him pay as he deserves, but I need to get her out of here so my men can do the *clean-up* once the building is empty.

We never leave traces. There's never a body left to be identified.

I reach the room that serves as a sort of storage and search for the secret door leading to the room where I ordered the man to be taken.

The basement is a multipurpose location for the *Syndicate*. Every fight venue has one and few people know of its existence.

Special *guests* are taken there. Mostly to be interrogated before they meet Satan, but the bastard won't have the chance to say anything in his defense. He's already dead, he just doesn't know it yet.

"Do you want me to take care of this?" Kellan asks, appearing at my side.

"No. Juno is mine; I'll handle him myself."

"In defense of the son of a bitch, he didn't know."

"From tonight on, everyone will know."

"Should I assume that based on today's experience, she's out of the fights?"

"Are you implying it's her fault?"

"Hey, calm down, brother. I'm a bastard one hundred percent of the time, but not a fucking caveman. He had no right to follow her even if she were completely naked."

"So what's your point here?"

"What I'm trying to say is that this won't be the first shit that happens to her, Cillian. The girl is like a damn temptation right in front of people's eyes. Even the most inexperienced man sees she's as fresh as a breeze. Pure, despite all the cocky attitude. We're not princes, nor are we amidst royalty's shit. She'll always be a problem. She's too pretty and *sexy*, and those eyes of hers promise paradise to a man."

"Watch yourself," I warn.

"I'm not going to touch her, fuck! I saw how you were looking at her in the ring."

I don't respond because anything I say will incriminate me.

"I'm going to talk to Aunt Orla to help her organize the damn bakery," I say. "I thought I'd have time to do that after she graduated, but apparently, not."

He stops with me at the door.

"Are you sure you don't want me to go in? There's still a fight going on upstairs and you won't be able to have fun with our guest. I've got the cleaning crew on standby, but you know it'll have to be quick."

"It will be. When I'm done, I'll take Juno to her place."

"You might want to know that the guy downstairs has a habit of violating women, regardless of their telling him *no*. I found out through some phone calls that various complaints against him in his company have been covered up in exchange for financial compensation."

"It doesn't matter to me. He could be a saint. After he assaulted her, his fate was sealed."

He makes no move to leave, so I enter the basement.

I descend the stairs, not caring at all about the musty smell and the dampness of the place.

The man probably doesn't know I'm coming yet, as there's another door at the bottom of the stairs.

I open it and see him pacing back and forth. I didn't order him to be tied up. He wouldn't have anywhere to go anyway.

"Cillian!" the bastard says as soon as I enter. "I was wondering when you'd show up. Your troglodytes don't know who I am and think they can lay a hand on me. I just wanted to have some fun, but those two bitches went crazy. It was self-defense. The crazy blonde hitting me with a heel and the other whore clinging to my back."

I close the door behind me, leaning against it.

"But you, unlike the others, know who I am," he says, trying to show some confidence, which we both know is a lie. I can smell his fear from a distance. "So, despite appreciating your hospitality, I need to go."

I still don't say anything, just assess him, trying to remember when we negotiated. There are so many faces, always the same in their arrogance, living in a bubble of power where they consider themselves untouchable, that I can easily confuse them.

I release the cuffs of my shirt and begin rolling up the sleeves to my elbows.

He looks and now doesn't even try to hide his terror, which confirms he at least has good instincts.

"Are you going to hurt me because of a whore?"

The voice comes out strangled, desperation replacing arrogance.

"Do you know who the woman you attacked is?"

"She told me she was your protégée, but only after..."

"You should have listened to what she said. Juno isn't just my protégée; she's a promise. The girl I swore to keep alive and safe."

"I didn't know she was important," he tries to justify himself.

"Forget it. She's none of your concern. Let's talk about you. At the beginning of this conversation, you said my men didn't know who you were. To be honest, neither did I. I've been trying to recall, but there are so many corrupt, thieving, fraudulent bastards who come through my hands that it's hard to remember them all." I walk towards him, and he looks back, trying to find an escape route.

There isn't one.

"You can't do this," he says, and I see in his eyes that he understands his time has come.

I walk over to one of the wall cabinets, where various weapons are laid out for our guests. I pick up a garrote with a steel ring at each end.

We both know he's going to die, and I think fear has paralyzed him to the point where he can't even argue anymore.

I circle around and position myself behind him. In one smooth motion, I wrap the steel wire around his neck, tightening it. I've done this so many times that I know the exact time it takes for a life to end, and within seconds, it's over. So fast he didn't even know what was happening.

"If you asked me who you are now, however, I'd say: a dead man."

Chapter 8

Cillian

I've never had problems handling these issues. Death is part of my daily routine. In our world, there are no second chances or space for forgiveness, but after dealing with that son of a bitch, I'm annoyed at having to go straight to find Juno.

Why? It's not like she's a nun. Even though she was raised sheltered, she's breathed the world of the *Syndicate* since birth. Although, when sent to Ireland, her contact wasn't as direct, she knows *who* we are and *what* we do.

Anyway, when I open the door to the room I left her in a few minutes ago, I feel uneasy when I find her sitting on the couch, head down, looking at her hands.

She probably knows I've arrived but doesn't look up.

Odhran is on the other side of the locker room, talking on the phone, giving me enough time to observe her.

She's still wearing the black corset and the stockings barely covering her legs. Juno is nothing like the pre-teen I took under my protection about ten years ago, but rather a sexual fantasy capable of arousing even the most apathetic of mortals. And I'm far from fitting into that group. I'm a healthy man with a frequent need for sex.

Her long blonde hair falls over her full breasts, forming a kind of curtain, partially hiding them from me, and I have to hold back the impulse to go over and push it aside to enjoy the view.

I know all the reasons why it's wrong to lust after her like this. That wasn't why I kept her safe all these years, but it's not something I can fight. The lust she ignites in me borders on madness.

She suddenly lifts her head but doesn't give any sign of noticing what's on my mind. However, I catch a movement in her throat as she swallows.

She's assessing me without even trying to hide, just as she did while strutting in the ring, and I'm experienced enough to understand what that look means. The physical attraction is mutual.

"The doctor has already examined her," Odhran says, but neither Juno nor I divert our gazes. "Now I have to go. Did you handle the *problem*?"

I know he's talking about the damn businessman.

"Yes."

"Alright. I did my babysitting, now I'll enjoy the rest of the night. See you around, sweetie," he says to Juno. "Try not to get into any more shit."

For the first time, I see a glimpse in her expression of what Kellan said, because if I had to guess, I'd say she was ready to give my brother a sassy reply.

"Are you okay?" I ask after he closes the door.

She shrugs.

"It's not the first time someone more than twice my size has hit me."

"What?"

She makes a move to stand, but I don't allow it.

"I didn't say you could leave, Juno. When we're talking, I'll let you know when you can leave."

I'm not joking, and I know she realizes it.

"Look, I think this first meeting is really weird, but I still want to say that I'm grateful for what you've done for me all these years, and I sincerely hope you kicked the ass of that fucker who hit me, but I'm not a child. Isn't having to ask for permission to leave a bit over the top?"

I study her face, thinking that maybe keeping her in a bubble, overly protected, hasn't done her any good. Maybe it's time she understands that I'm not her guardian angel.

"There are few people I respect in this world, Juno, and those I give such treatment to, I demand the same in return. You will never leave a place where we're talking until I'm done with the conversation. Am I clear?"

I see her pupils dilate and, perhaps unconsciously, she shifts on the couch. Seconds later, she nods.

"I didn't mean to offend you. I'm sorry."

"Tell me about it not being the first time you've been hit. Who did it? Your cousins in Ireland?"

"What? Of course not! They're like brothers to me."

"Who then? Your father?"

She studies my face, as if trying to decide whether to tell me the truth or not. It seems almost a minute passes before she finally responds:

"My father was the best man in the world. He would never lay a finger on me."

"Who then?"

"With all due respect, sir, but I'd need paper and a pen to jot down the list. I was very young, so it's hard to remember the endless list of my mother's lovers. Now, if you'll excuse me, I'd like to put on my clothes."

I'm still processing what she said and just nod, allowing her to dress.

Doireann, with several lovers? That bastard Oliver wasn't the first?

And then, more than the surprise at what she said, I focus on the tone of contempt with which she referred to her mother.

Quickly, a picture starts to form in my mind, and it's not a pretty one. In my arrogance, I thought I knew everything about Juno's childhood. I was sure Oliver was just a slip in Doireann's life, a needy woman who fell into the clutches of a seducer and paid with her life for it. However, Juno has just given me hints that her life was nowhere near what a regular girl would experience.

About five minutes later, she comes out of the bathroom dressed in jeans and a T-shirt.

Damn it, I hoped that removing the corset would reduce my reaction to her, but changing clothes made no difference. She's still delicious.

"Will the same driver who brought me take me back?" she asks.

"No. You're coming with me. Our conversation isn't over yet."

"I thought... um... I thought..."

"I'm not the kind of man who accepts half-truths, Juno. You told me you were beaten by your mother's lovers; I want to hear the whole story."

"Why, sir?"

"Just Cillian. You called me that on the phone."

"Because I had no idea what you were like in person."

"And what am I like in person?"

Another swallow, but she doesn't need to answer.

Her eyes reveal what she doesn't say: I affect her the same way she affects me.

However, there's something more. Despite our history, now that we're face to face, Juno isn't sure if she can trust me.

Chapter 9

Juno

I don't want to show how much everything that happened has shaken me, but I'm not that good an actress. That man attacking me brought back memories of a past I try to forget at all costs.

I'm no longer the girl who hid in the closet at home every time my mother had a *guest*. I'm an adult who knows how to defend herself and, if necessary, will die fighting.

However, alongside the craziness of the night, there's the fact that Cillian is incredibly intimidating.

What I feel near him is strange, because while my instincts scream that every cell of that man's body is dangerous, I also know that with him, I will always be protected.

"Where is Elaine?" I ask as we start walking toward the door.

He turns to look at me, his brow furrowing.

"Elaine?"

"The girl who helped me. She also works for you."

His face now shows recognition.

"Kellan sent someone to take her home."

"That man... Did he hurt her too?"

"He didn't have time."

The way he speaks tells me I shouldn't ask any more questions. Having grown up in this world, I know that if there's one thing to be said about the *Syndicate*, it's that they keep many secrets.

When we're outside in the corridor, I'm surprised to see it's completely empty, even though I can still hear the shouting of the crowd in the distance.

"Did you make everyone leave so we could pass?"

He stops again and stares at me.

"You ask too many questions."

"I can't help it. I'm naturally curious. Also, suspicious. I like to know where I stand."

"Haven't you figured out yet that you're safe with me? What happened today won't happen again, Juno. Now, let's get out of here."

Without waiting for a response, he places his hand on the small of my back, and I can't stop a shiver from running through my body.

I glance sideways, trying to see if he noticed, but Cillian would make an excellent poker player because his expression is completely void of emotion.

A few men follow us as we walk, and I know they are bodyguards. We're heading in the opposite direction from where I arrived, towards the back of the building. Probably because he doesn't want to walk through the crowd.

When we finally get outside, there's a driver waiting for us with the car door open. Not a chauffeur in the uniform and cap we see in movies, but one who could easily pass as one of my cousins: a nice guy mixed with a street fighter.

I get into the car and Cillian follows right after. I'm very nervous because the confined space creates an atmosphere of intimacy that makes my hands sweaty and my heart race.

I've always ignored men. I've exchanged a few kisses in school, of course, but never trusted enough to go a step further, especially since my cousins didn't give me much space to do so—if that's what I wanted—and it wasn't.

To give yourself to someone, you need to trust them, and there are few men who don't make me uncomfortable.

That said, one would expect my reaction to my protector to be the same as it's been with all men so far, but instead, I feel as if a magnetic bond is pulling me towards him.

I fumble a few times trying to fasten the seatbelt and know he's watching me, but he makes no attempt to help.

I mutter a curse under my breath, forgetting that I'm not alone, and finally manage to buckle it.

"You're not going to work in the fights anymore," he says, and if I were a sweet person, I would agree readily because, Jesus, the first experience was a horror movie. However, that would make me someone who easily bows her head, weak and unprotected, and I refuse to accept that role.

"Why? Do you think I provoked that man?"

I'm ready to argue if he says yes.

"No, but even so, you won't go back. I'll make sure your plans to open a bakery continue."

My heart pounds in my chest as I turn to face him. He had mentioned it before, of course, but I didn't think it would be so soon.

"What? But I don't know how to run a business."

I know these are the wrong words to say. I should thank him because hearing that is like having a dream almost within reach, but when I get nervous—and I am very nervous—I tend to fight back rather than just agree.

"Don't worry about that. I have qualified people to handle the administration."

"But I'm not qualified."

"Do you believe you're a good pastry chef?"

"I'm the best," I say without blinking. "My Aunt Eimear is the most honest person in the world and she used to say that my sweets are unparalleled."

"Then you already have the most important thing."

Even though I'm looking at him, he doesn't do the same, appearing interested in the scenery outside, even though it's a pitch-black night and there's nothing interesting to look at on the road.

"When do you plan to start this? My classes begin in a few weeks."

"I'll have someone check out some properties tomorrow. I'm also sure that my aunt will enjoy helping you with the process. She owns a restaurant, so she knows a lot about running that kind of business."

I know who he's talking about. Orla O'Callaghan, his father's sister-in-law. Cillian's and his brothers' lives are far from an open book, but I know the basics: that he was orphaned when both his parents were murdered by hired killers while he was still a teenager, and that this woman, Orla, is the one who raised them.

He doesn't seem very interested in interacting with me, but I'm not ungrateful, so my tongue itches to say what I want.

"Cillian."

He takes a while to meet my gaze again, but when he does, he invites me to dive completely into his eyes. He is, without fear of being wrong, the most intense person I've ever met.

"What is it?"

"Thank you. I don't know why you help and protect me so much. I believe it's because of my father, but even so, I wanted you to know that I'm grateful."

"Your father was a good soldier, but he's not the reason I took care of you. It was for Doireann, your mother. And that's why you'll tell me the whole story about how her lovers used to beat you."

Chapter 10

Cillian

"Do you mind if I put on some music, softly?" she asks as soon as we enter her apartment.

For a moment, I think I didn't hear the question correctly.

I was inspecting the place without any ceremony, checking out the rooms, including. All the while, she was behind me. Juno could have stopped me, but I think, given our previous conversation, she understands that I need to control every inch of my life. Checking that she's properly settled is part of the deal.

"What?"

"I don't know how to explain it."

"I'm listening."

"You make me nervous, and music calms me. If you want me to talk about the past without having a breakdown, I need some music. Some people drink to relax; I listen to music."

I stop in the hallway and look at her. The girl doesn't move, but I can feel the vibration coming from her. If she was already agitated over the phone, in person, she's ten times more. Juno seems like she has ants in her pants.

"Go ahead," I say, because anything is better than having her follow me so closely.

I'm not used to controlling my desires, and my body reacts hungrily to her presence.

Damn it. I have an endless supply of women more than willing to jump into my bed, and my dick wants the one I shouldn't even consider touching.

"And you can feel free to look around the rest of *my* apartment," she says, before leaving, with a subtle touch of irony.

I shake my head and for the first time tonight, I feel like laughing. The girl has a tongue full of thorns, but what usually irritates me in women, in her case, amuses me.

I continue walking, checking if the windows are secure enough, and after satisfying myself with what I see, I head back to the living room.

An instrumental music plays softly in the background, but it doesn't suit her at all, and maybe that's exactly what she was looking for: the calm of an apathetic song.

Juno is sitting, rigid, in an armchair relatively far from the others.

"Is this the kind of music you usually listen to?"

"No, but believe me when I say you wouldn't like it. Do you want something to drink?"

"No."

I should sit down too, but instead, I walk over to where she is. I stand in front of her and, on impulse, brush my thumb against her swollen cheek.

"Does it hurt?"

"No."

"Liar."

She doesn't pull away, so I move my finger to her cut lip.

"Why are you so prickly?"

"What's the point of showing weakness?"

Despite the harshness of her words, there's a latent fragility in her face. Juno is deconstructing the image I had of her. I treated her, I now realize, as a duty, but without truly caring about who she was or how her life was before her parents died.

"You're right," I agree. "You must hide your fear from everyone, but never from me."

Her face moves imperceptibly under my fingers, and the desire to hold it, to feel the silky skin, is so intense that I force myself to pull back, then sit down on the other side of the room.

"Tell me about your mother's friends."

"Friends? You mean the lovers? The men she cheated on Dad with?"

She drops the mask with that statement. It's easy to find pain in each of her words.

"You hated her," I state.

"Yes, and I think she got what she deserved."

If she had told me that a few years ago, it would have surprised me, but not anymore. What daughter would approve of her mother cheating on her father?

"But your father, didn't he?"

"No," she says, avoiding our eyes.

"Did he want your mother dead? Why did she betray your father, Juno?"

The corner of her mouth lifts, as if she's going to smile, but her blue eyes remain cold.

"Did I say I took care of you because of her? Well, I must be lucky, because if you had known the truth earlier, maybe you would have left me to my own devices."

"Why?"

"Because I was the one who told my father what she was doing. I wanted him to punish her."

"That wasn't just because of the betrayals."

"It was because of the betrayals *too*, but mainly because she made me scared all the time." She stands up, and I mirror her movement, approaching. "I think I've answered your questions, sir. She wasn't the loving mother you think. Not even close. She was a selfish, cruel bitch.

A monster who hated me above all else. Maybe now you regret it, because the girl you took care of all her life despises your precious friend, even after all these years when, I'm sure, she's long gone to hell."

I'm not the comforting type, but much more than her revelations, the despair in her words hits me deeply, as if a dagger were being twisted inside me.

Juno isn't pretending. That's pain in its most complete form.

I pull her into my arms, and she struggles. She punches my chest and tries to break free.

I don't allow it, because I don't want to let her go.

"I'm not going to hurt you. I will never hurt you," I repeat endlessly until she finally calms down.

Her arms come around my neck and hold on tightly, as if trying to merge with me.

Nothing about the girl is halfway. She's as intense as a storm. Nothing is lukewarm. She burns in my arms.

"Why do you care? You don't have to anymore. Now you know the truth."

"I'm not going to leave you alone, Juno."

"I'm a monster like she was."

"No, you're not."

As I hold her against me, I wonder how I could have been so wrong about Doireann, and the only possible answer is that I saw what I wanted to see. I clung to the memory of the girl from the past, and after she died, I held on to her to ease my guilt.

How much of my actions was responsible for what her mother did to Juno? Maybe I'll never know, but I'll spend the rest of my life ensuring that whatever she experienced in her parents' home is left behind.

"Tell me."

"No, I can't. But just be sure that I hate my mother, Cillian. I don't know who she was in your life, but I hate her and always will. That will never change."

Chapter 11

Cillian

I look out the window at the city of Boston beginning to wake up. By my standards, it's way too early to be here, but I barely slept a wink.

Last night, I stayed with Juno until she fell asleep.

I picked her up and carried her to her room. I didn't even know I was capable of taking care of a woman like that. The only women I've had any sort of loving contact with were my mother, Aunt Orla, and Doireann.

My jaw tightens when I think of the woman I defended even after she was dead. The one for whom I became an informal guardian to an orphaned girl, but who ultimately turned out to be a fucked-up freak who let the men she brought home abuse her daughter.

Juno didn't say anything more about her mother, but she cried herself to sleep.

My intuition tells me those weren't planned tears, but the tears of a lifetime.

She buried her face in the pillow, lying face down, but she didn't let go of my hand, and only when I was sure she was completely out did I leave.

I'm in my office, where, in theory, a virtual bank operates, but whose real operations the authorities don't even suspect. I'd be in prison if they did, but I'm very good at covering my tracks.

I asked Lorcan and my brothers to come see me because I need to know what really happened at Juno's house, and I'm not willing to wait until she wants to tell me.

I don't do things halfway and I'm going to find out what kind of hell she went through.

The door opens and the three of them walk in almost in sequence, my cousin with a cut on his mouth from the fight but smiling.

"Before you say anything, I won, as always."

I shake my head from side to side.

"Get ready to hear Aunt Orla scream on Sunday," I warn.

Our aunt goes crazy when he fights, and at our Sunday lunches, where we gather as a sort of tradition, she always lectures about the stupidity of men willingly getting punched.

"Nothing she doesn't do on a regular basis." He shrugs. "What's wrong? Why did you call us? I heard your girl got into trouble yesterday."

I've never spoken directly to him about Juno, but I'm not surprised he knows about her. I guess it's a fucking habit he picked up when he was an FBI agent. Lorcan misses nothing.

"It's already resolved, but I called you here for something related to Juno as well."

I quickly explain who Doireann was in my life and see the shock on my brothers' faces. Even though they were boys when I was already a teenager, I knew that mentioning Juno's mother's name would ring a bell. We were neighbors.

"So you took care of her because of her mother?" my cousin asks.

"Until yesterday, yes."

His brow furrows, but it's Odhran who speaks:

"What changed?"

"Everything. I don't know the details yet, but last night, when I left Juno at home, she broke down. I thought I was taking care of her because her father was my soldier, and when I touched on her mother's name and our old friendship, she fell apart in front of me."

I repeat word for word what she told me, including the beatings from her mother's lovers.

"Fuck, and where was her father, your man, letting this happen?"

"Out, probably," I reply. "Grady was nothing more than a soldier. He could be away for three, four weeks on a Union assignment."

It's not uncommon for soldiers to be sent on missions, especially when we're at war with another organization, which is almost always.

"Man, that's really fucked up. Bringing a lover into the house with the daughter present already makes your dead friend a bitch, but letting those bastards beat the girl..." Kellan growls. "Fuck!"

The room falls silent for a few seconds before Lorcan puts into words what we're all thinking. What *I* thought about the fucking whole night.

"And it was only physical abuse? I mean, beatings. Nothing more?"

I don't think so. The hatred Juno showed for her mother last night was too intense.

"I don't know, but I'll find out."

"For what? To confirm that her mother was a whore?"

"No. I don't need that confirmation. I believe Juno. The pain she showed yesterday was very real. She didn't want to tell me, but she exploded when she saw how wrong I was about who her mother was."

"If you're already sure the woman was worthless, then why do you want to find out if Juno's abuse went beyond beatings?"

"Revenge," I reply without hesitation. "Think about it. If Doireann had lovers, who were they? It's not like she could go out and party because Grady would find out, so she brought them into the house."

Kellan is the first to understand where I'm going with this.

"They were members of the *Union*."

"Yes, probably, or I would have found out, just as I eventually uncovered Oliver's identity, though it took years. If other names haven't come to light, it's because they were men who wouldn't raise suspicion if seen at Juno's parents' house."

"It makes perfect sense," my cousin says.

"I don't know what they did to her," I continue. "Whether they beat her or took her innocence, but everyone involved will pay."

"Wouldn't it be easier to ask your girl directly?" Kellan says.

"Maybe she doesn't even remember the names. She was a child. Besides, I think she only opened up yesterday because she was caught off guard about my friendship with her mother. Juno adored her father, from what I could see, and she felt she owed it to him that I took care of her. When she found out I did what I did for Doireann, she broke down."

"Man, I've seen a lot of shit in this world, but I'll never understand how parents can abuse or allow their children to be abused. Blood or not, children trust and depend on them. This shit is really fucked up," my younger brother says.

"I'll start the investigation, but it's been over ten years, right? There's a chance that her mother's old lovers might even be dead, if they were just soldiers," Lorcan continues.

"Yes, there is. And maybe, if they're lucky, they will be, because when I find out who hurt Juno, whatever the means, Oliver's death will seem like a walk in the park."

Chapter 12

Juno

I woke up feeling depressed.

Everything that happened yesterday came flooding back uncontrollably. I had no intention of exposing myself like that to Cillian. I don't remember ever doing anything like that in my entire life, even when I was a child and spent most of my time terrified.

I shattered into a thousand pieces, and my swollen eyes are proof of that.

Something broke the dam: the way he spoke about her, as if Doireann were someone admirable. As if she had been a good mother to me when, in reality, I grew up with only a father who, for the most part due to his work, wasn't home.

The funny thing is that, because of his way of economizing words in conversation, we never mentioned either of them, which made me believe that Cillian took care of me because of my father. The phone calls were just to check if I needed anything, and that was it, but I never had any idea that he believed I lived in a loving family.

I'm dying of embarrassment at how he saw me yesterday, but at the same time, relieved, because now there's someone else, besides my aunt, with whom I don't have to pretend to mourn the loss of my parents.

I grieve only for Dad. My hero. The one who, in an act of madness, ended my suffering.

I've just stepped out of the shower when my phone rings with an unknown number. I mean, all numbers, except for Cillian's and Aunt Eimear's, are unknown, so I answer, somewhat curious.

"Juno?" a woman's voice asks as soon as I say "hello."

"Yes, it's me. Who's speaking?"

"Orla O'Callaghan, Cillian's aunt. My boy said you want to open a bakery. Is that true?"

Jesus, what a direct person.

"Yes, it is."

"He also told me that you're the best baker there is, according to yourself. That sounds a bit pretentious, but I want to do a test. What's your specialty?"

All the depression I was feeling until a few minutes ago is replaced by the desire to show her that there's nothing pretentious about my claim, but that it's the absolute truth.

"I make some Irish sweets like Irish apple pie, *Porter cake*, *Mince pies*, and *Bailey's cheesecake*, but what I do best are *cupcakes*."

"Well then, let's start with your specialty. Make a list of what you need and send it to me. I'll be there in about an hour for the test."

"What? But I don't have anything, not even an ingredient!"

"That's why I asked for the damn list, girl. You're wasting time; almost a minute has passed."

"Are you serious? I've never tested my heart, and right now, it's about to jump out of my mouth. If this is a joke, I might die."

"All this drama over a little cake?"

"A little cake, no. The best *cupcake* you'll ever eat in your life!"

"We'll see. Get ready. I don't give compliments lightly."

IT'S ALMOST FOUR IN the afternoon now, and Cillian's aunt is sitting at my kitchen table, eating her third *cupcake* with a cup of tea in front of her.

I couldn't believe it when she told me to make a list, and as a sort of test, I asked for a professional mixer, which has always been my dream and that ten out of ten bakers say is the best.

I nearly fainted with excitement when she walked in with two security guards and everything I had asked for.

Is it possible to fall in love with an appliance? Because I'm having an intense love affair with this mixer.

From our conversation while preparing the *cupcakes*, I realized that she's not just a restaurant owner but is used to getting her hands dirty, literally. However, she never offered to help me. She said she was seeing if I was truly talented or just conceited.

My self-esteem isn't the best, but if there's something I do well in life, it's baking.

The woman, however, is tough as nails. She wasn't joking when she said she didn't give compliments lightly, but after tasting my dessert for the third time, I think it's pretty obvious she liked it.

"You have talent," she says finally, and I feel like I've won a cooking contest.

Orla O'Callaghan is nothing like gentle; she's almost a female version of her older nephew, and yet, I felt an immediate connection with her.

"I told you," I say without any modesty. "You'll never eat a *cupcake* as good as this in your life."

"Wrong answer, young lady. You should say, '*Thank you, ma'am. I'm honored that you enjoyed my work.*'"

"If I did that, I wouldn't be myself."

"And are you always yourself?"

"No. Usually not, which is why I wanted to come back to the United States."

"To stay away from your family and stop pretending?"

During the time I was cooking, she eventually asked me one question or another, though I'm almost certain she knows a lot more about me than she lets on.

"Something like that. I'm very grateful to my aunt who finished raising me, but it's time to stand on my own."

She looks at me in silence for so long that it makes me anxious.

"Is it a family trait?"

"What are you talking about, girl?"

"These silences. Mad Lion and Cillian did this to me, and now you."

"I was thinking about your statement and whether it was too early to burst your bubble."

"I'm not sure I understand."

"Cillian considers you his own, Juno. You'll never walk on your own without the entire *Sindicato* protecting you."

My damn heart shouldn't be beating like this, but who said I can stop it?

Then, I remember last night and deflate like a balloon that's just been popped.

He didn't take care of me. He did what he did to fulfill a promise to Doireann.

"Want more *cupcake*?" I change the subject.

"Oh God, no. If I eat another sweet, I'll be heading straight to the emergency room, but I'd like us to have lunch next week to discuss business. I'll see you on Tuesday at my restaurant."

Her phone rings, and the name she calls makes my heart race once more.

"Yes, I'm here with Juno, Cillian. You should come try the *cupcake* your protégée makes. It's a piece of heaven."

They talk for a few more minutes, and I pretend to clean the dishes I've dirtied, but I'm actually listening intently to every word. But it's when she hangs up that I nearly have a heart attack.

"He's coming up."

"What?"

"He was already downstairs, and it seems I convinced him to come try your sweets. All my boys have a sweet tooth."

After she says this, she stands up and grabs her purse.

"Are you leaving?"

"Yes, I have to stop by the restaurant."

To my surprise, she comes over to where I am and pulls me into her arms. Orla is a small, petite, and slender woman, and the difference between us is almost ridiculous, but even so, when she hugs me, I feel so good. It's comforting, as if she were used to doing it all the time, and I find myself wondering if her boys allow themselves to be hugged easily.

"Don't forget our appointment on Tuesday, Juno." She walks to the door. "Or better yet, what are you doing on Sunday?"

"I don't have any plans, to be honest. I was thinking of going to Boston Harbor."

"Leave it for the following week. Come have lunch with me. My boys will be there too."

"Are you sure about this?"

"Yes. No one should eat alone on Sundays. That's against my rules."

I smile at her bossy manner, almost as bossy as her "boys."

"Let me at least bring the dessert."

"Okay, but if you're going to make *cupcakes*, calculate at least half a dozen times four, not counting mine. Those boys, when they get together, don't mess around."

I accompany her to the door, but when I open it, I come face to face with the only man to date who has the power to make my heart skip a beat.

Chapter 13

Cillian

I t's not uncommon for me to be attracted to women, and I don't have a specific type. The term *sexually active* doesn't even begin to cover me. I rarely go more than two days without getting laid.

Sex is like a kind of fuel. A nourishment I need to relax from the madness that is my life. However, one thing to be said about me is that when I want a woman, I become obsessed with her and ignore all others.

When I was on my way here, lying to myself that I was just going to check her out, I thought I should have accepted the brazen invitation from one of the lawyers who handles the legal side of my business, with whom I've been with a few times.

She's a satisfactory occasional lay, and I could have used that to kill or at least dull the effect Juno has on my body. But despite the woman making it clear that I could fuck her on my desk, my cock didn't even twitch.

Now, however, as I say goodbye to my aunt and watch her leave and shut the door behind me, I let my eyes roam over my protégée's body, and the desire that overwhelms me is almost painful.

Damn, she's beautiful. Not just the breathtaking combination of a perfect body, long legs, and full breasts that resemble ripe fruit. Or her long blonde hair, those confident blue eyes surrounded by lashes that look made up, and that watch me unflinchingly.

There's a *something more* about the girl that I can't quite define, but that moves me deeply. An irresistible, silent call that sets my blood on fire.

She stares at me, her lips slightly parted, the lower one a bit fuller, making me want to bite it until I hear her moan.

Juno's presence leaves me dazed. The effect she has on me borders on out of control.

I'm a guy who doesn't allow himself to be overtaken by emotion, not even during sex, but at this moment, if I were to follow my instincts, I'd strip her naked here, standing up, and mark every inch of her body with my tongue.

She's wearing a simple, strappy dress, and if I were to bet, without a bra. Maybe the air conditioning in the apartment is too strong because her nipples, which I can see are large through the outline of the fabric, are perfectly visible against the dress, almost like a second skin.

"Cillian, I didn't know you were coming."

I didn't either.

I mean, I told the driver to bring me to her neighborhood, but I was still resisting the idea of seeing her again. I knew my aunt was here and Orla gave me the perfect excuse to come up.

"I came to try your sweets."

For the first time since I saw her in person after her return to Boston, Juno smiles.

"I don't know if I want to share. That whole cook-not-tasting-their-own-food thing doesn't work for me. I'm greedy."

Holy shit, the girl has no idea of the dirty thoughts her words have brought to my mind. How much I'd like to push that greed to the limit to see where we could go.

Fuck me, I feel like a teenager with a hard-on around her.

"The best pleasures are always shared, Juno. Don't you know that yet?"

She moistens her lips, and I follow the movement of her pink tongue.

"Are they? I don't know anything about that and I'm not very good at sharing anything."

"Then I guess I'll have to teach you."

She doesn't back away; instead, she shows me signs of how much fire lies beneath her innocence.

"You don't seem like the sharing type either."

I fall silent, trying to guess if we're talking about the same thing, but I come to the conclusion that we're not.

What the hell am I thinking? Juno is just a girl.

Besides, that's not why I came here.

Why did I come here, to begin with?

Yesterday.

Focus on what happened yesterday, when she broke. Focus on the pain and the past, and maybe the urge to have her will diminish.

She offers her hand.

"Come, I'll feed you. I wasn't serious about not sharing. — She smiles. — Not *too* serious, anyway."

I intertwine our fingers, but instead of letting her guide me, I pull her close, maybe with a bit too much roughness, because our bodies press together. I should push her away, but the problem is that after feeling the warmth of her skin, I want more.

"Did you sleep well?"

She doesn't look at me.

She shrugs.

"Thank you for staying yesterday. I didn't plan to put on that *show*."

"One day, I want to hear the full story."

"I don't like to remember the past."

"Look at me." She obeys. "I don't know what happened, but there's nothing to be ashamed of. You were just a kid."

"Why did she hate me so much?"

The last conversation I had with her mother comes back to my memory.

It couldn't have been because of what I told her. That would be too sickening.

"Cillian?"

"I don't have an answer for that, Juno. I had no idea she was being mistreated at home."

"It doesn't matter. I just wanted to say *thank you* for yesterday. Now, come try those *cupcakes*. I'll show you why investing in my bakery is the best deal in the world. Have a seat."

She goes to the counter, while I settle into a chair at the small table, which, for my size, feels like a dollhouse.

"What flavor do you want?"

"What do you have to offer?"

"Blueberries, chocolate, and..."

"Chocolate" I reply without blinking.

She's smiling as she starts walking toward me with a *cupcake* in hand.

"Your aunt ate three. She said you and your siblings have a sweet tooth" she says, playfully holding the treat in front of me, but not handing it over. "Is that true?"

"Exaggeration." I dismiss it, but the smell of the treat is making my mouth water.

Or maybe it's imagining the sweet *on her* that makes me want to eat it.

"Really? Then if I do this" she says, running her index finger along *my* cupcake and bringing it to her mouth "you wouldn't mind?"

Before she can taste it, I grab her wrist and bring the finger smeared with frosting to my mouth.

The mix of her flesh with the sugary frosting is fucking aphrodisiac, and all I want is to strip her naked and spread that cream all over her body.

I let her go before I do something stupid.

"Gave up?" she asks, but her breath shows that she knows we're not playing anymore.

"You're just a girl, Juno, and I understand that the biggest responsibility for being so inexperienced falls on me. I was the one who decided you should be raised in a protective bubble. On the other hand, I'm not a guy you could flirt with. Don't start something you can't finish."

Chapter 14

Cillian

She's trembling, but she doesn't pull away.

I want her to. I need her to reject me and say it's wrong because she's just a girl I should protect, not desire naked beneath me, moaning and whining while I bury myself in her.

"I don't know what it would be like to *go all the way*," she says, tempting me even more. "I've only ever kissed."

I know that, of course, but hearing the proof of her inexperience from her own mouth excites me like hell.

I stand up and face her. She's tall, but still a good twenty centimeters shorter than me.

"You can't handle me, Juno. I'm not the kind of man a woman should dream about. I don't plan for the future because it's uncertain and may never happen. I don't nurture dreams or desires. I fuck and then I leave. You told me you're inexperienced, and I know you're telling the truth, but you can't be so naive as not to understand when a man wants you. I want you, but if I make you mine, I'll hurt you. So, be a good girl and offer me only what will be painless for you: your sweets."

She steps back as if I had attacked her, and that's for the best. The sooner Juno realizes I'm not a fucking Prince Charming, the sooner she can run away.

"Do you want something to drink with the cake?" she asks, placing the treat in front of me, without making eye contact.

"No. I like to savor each pleasure separately until I've extracted everything I can from it, and for that, I dedicate myself to one at a time."

She takes a deep breath and leans against the sink as if she needs to keep herself from moving.

We're two.

The sweet, which looks damn good, has become a mere supporting actor. My hunger now is different.

"Your face has de-puffed," I say, sitting back down.

"It's better now. Your aunt didn't say anything about it. I know she noticed because my mouth is cut, but she didn't ask why. Does she know what happened in the fight?"

I notice she doesn't ask me what I did with the businessman.

"Probably. I didn't say anything, but maybe one of the guys did."

"Aren't you going to eat?"

Without breaking eye contact, I finally taste the *cupcake*.

"Damn" I groan as the sweet frosting hits my tongue.

She almost smiles, pleased, because I'm sure she knows how good her dessert is.

"I analyzed what you said about opening the bakery and I think instead of diversifying like I originally thought, after talking with your aunt, I'll specialize only in *cupcakes*. One day, I'm going to sell them nationwide."

"Do you love cooking that much?"

I just ate, but I can't stop myself from licking the rest of the sweet off my thumb. The woman works magic with sugar. I've never tasted anything so delicious.

She shrugs.

"I haven't had much to dedicate myself to in my life besides family, school, and sweets."

"That's not what I asked."

"Yes, I love cooking."

Suddenly, something I hadn't thought of occurs to me.

"Do you resent how you were raised? For me having overprotected you?"

"No. I never really wanted to see the world outside my aunt's gates. For the first time, I had a real family. They loved me and never stopped saying so, not even the boys. I never felt like an intruder or like I didn't belong."

"So why did you want to come back?"

"Because one day, my aunt won't be with us anymore. My cousins will have their own families, and I would have to leave anyway. I don't handle rejection well, even when it's forced by circumstances. So, I preferred to choose the moment to say goodbye rather than be forced to do it."

"That's very heavy for someone so young to say."

"Most girls my age didn't have the same kind of childhood I did. I'm not a normal girl; I'm a survivor."

"I want to know everything."

"For what? We're nothing to each other." Her voice betrays no emotion. It's empty and hopeless. "There will come a time when you'll realize that I'm big enough and don't need protection. There will come a time when you'll have your own life. A wife and kids. Do you think any woman will accept the shadow of another, even if that other is nothing more than a ward, beside her?"

"I'm not planning to get married, and even if I were, that has nothing to do with us."

She turns her back and starts washing the dishes in the sink.

"Juno."

"Do you want me to put some of the *cupcakes* in a container for you to take with you? There are still plenty left."

I move to where she is and, knowing it's the wrong move, pin her against the sink, pressing myself against her back. One arm on each side.

Immediately, her scent awakens me, and I know I should pull away, but I don't move.

Juno turns, and our faces are very close now. Mine over hers.

"I don't need your pity. I will always be grateful, but I'd rather lose an arm than be kept close to someone out of pity."

A muscle of tension tightens my jaw, such is the force I use to keep myself from taking what I want from her.

"It has nothing to do with pity, but because you've become a part of my life. You're right when you say that if I had a wife, she wouldn't want you near me, because only being dead would make someone not realize how much I desire you."

Until the last second before crushing my mouth against hers, I still try to fight, knowing that the moment I touch her, the battle will be lost. But Juno doesn't resist. Instead, she parts her lips, eagerly awaiting my next move.

Then, I take what I've wanted since the moment I saw her in the ring yesterday. I hold her perfect face and run my finger over the still-swollen side. I bring my mouth close, licking her tempting lower lip, savoring the silky touch. I invade her, exploring every corner of her warm mouth, beckoning her tongue to dance, moving inside her.

Chapter 15

Cillian

Her hands come to my hair, and she doesn't hesitate in her submission. Maybe, and this is just a damn *maybe*, if Juno were to show some shyness, there might be a slight chance I would back off, but she's hungry too, and she kisses me back as if she wants me as much as I want her.

Her sensuality is almost sinful, irresistible. I want to touch every part of her. To take her and corrupt her innocent body, teaching her how much pleasure we can give each other.

I grab her ass and press our bodies together. My hard cock grinds against her abdomen, but it's not enough. As I'm about to lift her to feel her sex pressed against mine, my phone rings.

We both jump. The reality of what was about to happen hitting us both.

She pulls away from me and finally steps back.

Without looking away from her, I answer my cousin's call.

"What's happened?"

"I have a lot of information about your protégé's mother's past."

"Where are you?"

"At Aunt Orla's restaurant. Can you come meet me?"

"All right. I'll see you in half an hour."

I hang up the phone, and she's still looking at me but has kept her distance. Her left hand touches her lower lip, which I sucked and licked.

There's something about the way her fingers wander over her skin that makes me feel filthy next to her purity.

"I need to go."

"I'll have the guys take the *cupcakes*... uh... I'll have them delivered wherever you live."

I move closer, and her breathing becomes irregular once again.

"What I did with you shouldn't have happened, but I don't regret it. From the moment I saw you in the ring, thoughts of having you naked in my bed, moaning while I fuck you hard, invaded my mind. But you need to know what you're getting into. I'm not looking for love."

Her chin lifts and her posture stiffens.

"I'm not looking for love either, nor the kind of relationship you must be used to having with your women. I need nothing more than my plans for the future, my bakery. I'll take you to the door. From what I understand, you have an appointment now, sir."

I stare at her, still unmoving. I know I've hurt her by putting her on the same level as all the others I date, but she needs to know who *I* am.

My mind knows I need to leave, but my body still hesitates. Finally, reason wins.

My bodyguards are in the hallway and accompany me to the car, only then getting into the vehicles they arrived in.

The building where she lives is mine. It's only six floors, two apartments per floor, and all the occupants were vetted, or I would never have allowed her to live here.

Still, I wonder if I should have moved her closer to my house, or even given her the choice to live in one. I thought for a single girl, the apartment would be a good option, but now that I know a bit more about Juno, she doesn't seem to fit, with all that energy radiating from her delicious body, in an apartment. It's like keeping a beautiful bird caged.

"Isn't that what she is?" my conscience screams. *"A beautiful and exotic bird you hesitate to set free?"*

Juno talked about my future. I'm Irish, so of course, I want a family, preferably a big one, but even though I know she's right about what she said, that no woman would want someone as beautiful as her around me, I can't imagine living a life without knowing if Juno is being well taken care of and protected. Without constantly checking on her.

As my driver drives, I look at the streets of Boston through the darkened windows of the vehicle, trying to understand when things got so complicated.

"When you saw her", a voice whispers.

My father used to tell us a story that from the moment he laid eyes on my mother for the first time, he knew she would be his only one.

It's a legend, a kind of superstition told and retold by the men in our family, that says our chosen one is already determined and there's nothing we can do to fight it.

It's certain that no woman to date has gone as deep into me as Juno has, and the madness seems even greater, given that I've done nothing but kiss her.

I rest my head back and close my eyes.

No way she's the right woman for me.

When I took her under my domain and responsibility, it was solely to make up for the tragedy that happened in her young life.

From every angle I look at it, getting involved with Juno feels wrong, especially because, in the end, I'll end up hurting her.

When we finally park in front of Aunt Orla's restaurant, I'm relieved to be able to occupy my mind with something other than the memory of the blonde goddess. Of her moist, swollen lips from the kisses we exchanged. Of how her body molded against mine as if we were two pieces searching for the perfect fit.

"How many *cupcakes* did you eat?" Aunt Orla asks as soon as I enter.

I lean down to kiss her forehead.

"Just one."

"So, what were you doing there all this time?"

"How do you know I was still there?"

She doesn't answer, and I consider the matter closed. There's no point in lying, since she is one of the people who knows me best.

"Don't mislead the girl, Cillian. I had a different idea of her, based on who her mother was, but I had to swallow my prejudice today."

"What does that mean?"

"I never liked Doireann. It wasn't exactly a secret."

I already suspected that, because my aunt is incapable of giving someone a kiss if she doesn't like their face.

"Why didn't you like her?"

"Sneaky, deceitful. Even very young, she behaved with people according to what she thought they expected from her."

"Doireann was my friend when I needed her."

She stood by me when my parents were murdered. When I didn't even want my family around.

"Because she thought she'd have a chance to win you over. It's amazing that someone as perceptive as you couldn't see her true interests."

What she says aligns with what happened years later, at our last meeting, but at the time, I thought she was just bored with the marriage and didn't take her seriously.

"Anyway, it's Juno I want to talk about. The girl is good. I've never been wrong about a human being before. Juno is a good girl, and one day, some lucky person will notice that and take her for themselves, so don't mislead her. Don't make her dream of a future with you if that's not what you want."

Chapter 16

Cillian

As I walk toward the table where my cousin is sitting at the back of the restaurant, Aunt Orla's words dominate my thoughts.

"Juno is a good girl, and someday, some lucky guy will notice that and take her for himself."

Shouldn't hearing that bring me relief?

So why does the thought of another man kissing that mouth, tasting her body, make me want to kill someone?

I don't have much time to think about it because my cousin is coming toward me.

"Your face looks like shit."

"I'm in a bad mood."

"As usual."

"What did you find out?"

"Let's go to the back, to the office. I've done more than *find out.* I have one of the men who... um... *visited* Juno's mother at one of our warehouses."

We sit in the room Aunt Orla uses to run her business.

There's no risk of us being overheard here because the place undergoes a sweep three times a day.

"Speak."

"You were right. From what I could gather, Doireann's lovers... Was that the name of the bitch? Her lovers were all members of the *Syndicate*, except for Oliver Wilson."

74

"How did Grady not suspect him?" I ask, trying to avoid the main issue and not focus, for now, on the fact that several of my men might have hurt Juno.

"Grady was after a divorce. He hired Oliver as his lawyer to help him get custody of Juno, and since Doireann spread her legs for anyone, it's no surprise she did so with the lawyer representing her husband too."

"Okay. He might have been divorcing her upon discovering the infidelity, but then why kill her? Even if he had caught her with Oliver, which I know wasn't the case if my theory is correct, it's not something he wouldn't have already known. Why end her life and then take his own, knowing it would leave Juno orphaned?"

"To get that answer, you need to come with me to the warehouse, where one of the soldiers confessed the whole story. It's not pretty, Cillian. It's a lot more fucked up than we thought."

"How many of my men were involved?"

"Many, I suppose, but as we suspected, most of them are already dead. He didn't give me all the names because he probably doesn't know them either, but from what I could check, he was the only one left."

"Take me to the son of a bitch."

I KNOW WHO HE IS, BUT I couldn't remember his name. On the
way here, however, Lorcan gave me his entire file.

Rick Collins.

Although he has spent several years working for me in the New
York crew, he has been with the *Syndicate* since I took over, when my
uncle, our former leader, died.

He must be a bit older than me, in my thirty-eight. I think he's
about the same age as Doireann.

When I arrive at the warehouse, he is almost unrecognizable. Most
of my men don't like child abusers in any sense. We Irish value family.

"Start talking," I warn as I approach.

"Boss..." he tries.

"For now, I'm still your boss, you piece of shit." I crouch in front of
him. "How long have you been with me?"

"My whole life."

"Then you know you can make this worse or better for yourself,
depending on how quickly you give me the information I want."

He looks at me and knows I'm serious.

"The bitch was crazy. Doireann. I don't know what the hell Grady
saw in her. Or rather." He pauses and spits some blood. "I know. All that
brown hair and those incredibly sweet eyes. A provocative body, but
totally empty of soul."

For the second time in less than twenty-four hours, I hear someone
speak of the woman I loved like a sister, with no sexual interest, as
someone cruel. In both instances, it was hard for me to connect the
image of Doireann I knew with a nasty bitch.

Then I remember Juno's tears. The suffering and outrage that even
today, after so many years of her death, she still feels for her mother, and
I understand that it's all true.

"What went on in that house?"

"Before I tell you, I want you to know that I had no idea how far
she would go."

"Don't bullshit me, fucker."

"I can only speak for myself. There were many others, though, but I can't say if they were before or after. At first, it was regular sex. She was always drunk and was fun. Didn't care if the girl could hear us."

Jesus Christ.

"The third time I went, she asked me out of the blue to beat her daughter so she could watch. I resisted at first, but she gave a blowjob like no one else, so I ended up giving in. I didn't hit her hard," he closes his eyes "but I'll never forget the girl screaming and asking what she had done to deserve that."

I land a punch that breaks his nose.

Maybe he was already expecting it, because despite the scream of pain, he doesn't complain.

"She hated her daughter. Don't ask me why, but she hated the girl with all her might. The last time I went, which was the last straw for me, the child seemed strangely quiet and smelled of alcohol."

I feel my blood boil.

"How do you know that? You would have had to get very close to be sure."

"When I saw her unconscious, I was afraid she was dead. I've done a lot of shit in my life, but I've never killed a child."

"No. Just beat her," I say, each word dripping with all my hatred.

He nods.

"The girl was drunk that last time. If I had to guess, I think Doireann made her drink alcohol for what she had in mind."

"And what was that?"

"She wanted me to molest the daughter while she watched. I wasn't supposed to rape her, but do things... that shouldn't be done to children. She said I couldn't go all the way, because if I did, the girl would feel pain and the father would find out."

"Motherfucker, bitch!"

I wish she were alive so I could kill her myself. I want to see the life drain from those deceiving eyes.

"I left. I wouldn't even have sex with an adult woman if she was unconscious, boss. I would never do such fucked-up shit to a child. But I think there were others after me. I don't know what they did to her."

I grab my gun and his eyes widen. He's of no use to me anymore. The other names Lorcan got from the fucker are all of dead men.

"I've told you everything. Don't I deserve a second chance?"

"I don't know that concept, but I'll give you a quick death."

I fire a single bullet between his eyes and then turn my back on him. My brothers and cousin are waiting for me outside.

"I need to make sure there aren't any more of these motherfuckers alive," I say. "If there are, I'll take them one by one."

Chapter 17

Juno

I lean against the door as soon as he leaves, my heart still racing.

How can I be so stupid? Even after everything he told me, showing me how he treats women, I still want him.

I never thought I'd trust a man enough to let him get to a greater intimacy, but when Cillian kissed me, holding me against his hard, muscular body, I wanted him to touch me all over.

It just felt right that he touch and taste me.

How can I, in such a short time, surrender like this?

"Because you've known him almost your whole life," a voice says.

Even from a distance, he has been, along with what was left of my family, my safe harbor for years.

What happened today, however, has definitively changed our relationship. Cillian is no longer just my protector, but the one I want to be my first everything.

I want to learn to surrender. To know what it's like to be touched by someone I desire, in an equal situation, and not to be subjected, as almost happened in my early adolescence.

I sit on the floor and hug my knees.

How is it possible that I didn't feel anything until today, not even for the boys at school whom I allowed to kiss me, and now, just his presence makes me tremble and desire to be possessed?

The cell phone rings and when I get up to answer it, I see it's from an unknown number — another one.

"Hello?"

"Juno? It's Elaine. I asked Kellan for your number because I wanted to check if you're okay."

"Elaine, hi! Oh, I thought about you a lot today, but had no idea how to find you. They took you home yesterday, right? Are you okay?"

"Yes, I'm fine. That son of a bitch didn't hurt me. What the hell happened, exactly?" She pauses. "Wait, tell me what you're doing. Do you want to go out for a burger tonight?"

"Sure. It's the first time someone has invited me out since I arrived."

"Where shall we meet?"

"Could it be a little earlier? A snack instead of dinner? I'm still a bit sore from last night and don't want to stay up late. Also, I'll need to use some makeup to cover up the damage on my cheek."

"That's fine. Do you want me to come by?"

I think about the security and how I could explain to her that I have a mini-army taking care of me.

"No. Just tell me where to find you."

"It's a more remote neighborhood, but it's neutral as well."

"Neutral?"

"Honey, I don't know who you are, but I know you're someone important to the royalty" she says, I think referring to the *Syndicate*. "The boss and the middle brother went crazy when they entered the locker room and saw you passed out. So I'm not stupid enough to take you to a neighborhood dominated by another organization."

Oh, I see now what she meant by *neutral*.

"Alright. Send me the address by text, but allow an hour for me to be able to meet you."

"THIS PLACE IS REALLY nice," I say, looking around the restaurant.

"Isn't it? I don't come here often because, for my standards, it's a bit expensive, but at least we'll be away from any trouble. Now tell me: who are you?"

"A half-Irish, half-American girl who came back to the United States after ten years away."

"Wow, that sounds exciting. Is it true that Irish people are great lovers?"

"Jesus!" I laugh at her cheekiness, but then I feel my cheek twitch.

She notices and curses out the man who assaulted us yesterday.

"It's a shame they took him away. I wanted to beat him myself," she says.

"I'm with you on that."

"Tell me what happened yesterday."

"Nothing. I walked into the locker room, he followed me, and didn't accept a refusal."

"I hate those rich assholes who think they can pay for anything. Well, I'm sure he was properly punished..."

She says that as if asking a question.

"I couldn't say. — I look at her, trying to figure out how to say what I need without being rude. — I'm glad you invited me to dinner, Elaine..."

"But?"

"If you invited me to talk about Cillian or the guys, I'm leaving."

"I didn't, I swear. I've been working in fights for a while. I try to stay out of trouble. I'd be lying if I said I'm not curious about your relationship with the elite, because those four bodyguards sitting two tables away don't even pretend they're not ready to rip my head off if they think you're in danger, but I really invited you because I was worried about you yesterday. You were completely out cold."

"That bastard had a heavy hand."

"I believe it. The man was big, a damned coward."

I look at her with curiosity. She seems well-experienced.

"You asked me... uh... if Irish people are great lovers. You said you've been working in fights for a while. Have you ever dated one?"

"No. I stick to the belief that you don't eat where you make your bread. I wasn't born to be a name crossed out in some guy's notebook. I'm going to have a future that doesn't involve being almost naked in the middle of a bunch of beer-stinking ogres."

"So why the curiosity?"

"Just because I don't date one doesn't mean I don't fantasize, right?"

I laugh, and again the damn cheek hurts.

"Aren't you going back to fighting?" she asks.

"No. No offense, but last night was more than enough."

I don't go into details about my pastry work or anything related to Cillian or his family. Even if I had known her for a long time, which is not the case, I was taught from a young age that any topic related to the *Syndicate* should stay between us.

"You said you came back from Ireland, and considering how many people are taking care of you, you must be important to the boss's family, but do you plan to stay locked up at home day and night?"

"I'm going to work," I say vaguely, "and my classes start again in two weeks. I'm in my final term of Gastronomy."

"Wow. Now I'm impressed. What do you like to cook? What's your specialty?"

"Sweets."

We talk so much that, little by little, I manage to relax, and I end up forgetting what I said about planning to go to bed early.

Two *milkshakes* and a burger with fries later, I remember that the bodyguards are probably hungry too.

I know they won't eat while I'm here because on the first days, when I went out for a walk, they didn't accept anything I offered. I think they must take turns when they're watching over me at home.

Wow, what a boring job.

"I have to go. They must be starving," I say, nodding toward the men.

She asks for the check, and as I walk to the bathroom, my cell phone rings.

I shiver when I see who it is.

"Cillian."

"Juno, what time do you plan to say goodbye to your friend?"

"How do you know that... — Of course, the bodyguards. — I'm leaving now. I didn't know there was a curfew, sir. My mistake," I say, half-joking, half-annoyed.

To my surprise, the voice that answers is much softer than it usually is. Softer by his standards, of course.

"I just want to make sure you'll be safe."

I grip the phone tightly, feeling tears well up in my eyes.

"Don't do this," I ask.

"Don't do what, Juno?"

"I got your message today. You see me as a duty, regardless of Doireann, but don't make me believe you care about me."

He doesn't respond, and I hang up without saying goodbye.

What did Aunt Eimear say? *No answer is already an answer.*

Chapter 18

Juno

On Sunday

"**A**unt, I'm going to have lunch at Cillian's family's house."

"What?" Her question comes out so high-pitched that I have to pull the phone away from my ear for a moment.

Jesus.

"His aunt invited me to the weekly family lunch. It's not like I have a thousand other plans waiting, so I said *yes*."

I'm downplaying how excited I was about Orla's invitation. If there's one thing I miss about Ireland, it's the meals shared with my cousins on weekends. They only missed out if they were out of town, otherwise, they found a way to show up.

Having been an only child and my family being far from regular, I learned to value these gatherings with Aunt Eimear's kids.

"Don't you think you're getting too close to the eye of the storm, dear?"

"I've always been in the eye of the storm. I was born into it, remember?"

It's strange that she's so resistant to my getting closer to Cillian and his family, considering it was the man who supported me all these years.

I also don't want to throw in her face that Orla and the nephews are no different from her and my cousins. The only thing that distinguishes them is that Cillian and his brothers are part of the Irish mafia elite, while my cousins are soldiers.

"I know that. I think I'm overreacting, but I still can't come to terms with my little girl living alone in a strange city."

I roll my eyes, though I partially understand her concern. But it annoys me a bit that she's so overprotective just because I'm a woman. Her children live on their own, and one of them even left home at eighteen, and she never tried to dissuade him.

I can't deny that she's right to worry, being my aunt. Putting myself in her place, I'd feel the same way. What bothers me is that every time I tell her what I'm going to do, there's a "but" to add.

Determined not to argue, I change the subject.

"Orla is going to help me set up the pastry shop."

"Now it's all 'Orla this, Orla that.' I'm starting to feel jealous."

"Don't be silly, no one will ever take your place in my heart."

And it's true. For all intents and purposes, Aunt Eimear was the only mother I ever had.

"Just kidding, my love. I'm glad you're finding your own way. It's hard to see the kids grow up, but I'm very proud of every one of your achievements."

"I haven't achieved anything yet, but I will soon, God willing. Now I have to go because I don't want to be late. Kisses to you and the boys."

I look at myself one last time in the mirror before leaving the apartment, but my mind isn't on the image in front of me, it's miles away. My heart races just knowing I'll see him soon.

In one thing, Aunt Eimear was right, even though she doesn't know about the strong physical attraction between me and Cillian: I'm very close to the eye of the storm.

Yes, because that's what this hunger he awakens in my body, previously unknown, is.

A storm. Intense, furious, uncontrollable.

I don't want to be a toy in his hands. I won't accept giving myself to a man for the first time and end up being just a mere amusement.

When I'm near my protector, I feel on the edge of a cliff: the height terrifies me, but the excitement of the jump urges me to leap.

I take a deep breath, thinking about how I should behave today, but I know it doesn't depend on my will. My body seems to have a life of its own around him.

TWO AND A HALF HOURS later, lunch at Orla's house is officially over.

To my embarrassment, by the time I arrived, everyone was already at the huge two-story mansion.

I didn't even need to be a genius to guess that Cillian's aunt hadn't informed him, his two brothers, or his cousin, who is no less intimidating than the other male relatives, that I was coming.

I had to use all my rather poor skill at camouflaging my emotions to avoid showing the intense urge to run away.

I greeted them with a nod, as if they were ordinary people and not the Irish mafia elite, and then I made my way to the lady of the house.

She was oblivious to my discomfort and, thank God, was kind enough to ask me to help her in the kitchen, as she dismissed the staff on Sundays. Getting away from Cillian for a bit gave me time to calm down.

The whole house is very impressive, with its expensive-looking furniture and carpets that, if I had to guess, I'd say are Persian because they resemble those seen on celebrity TV shows. Every time a presenter mentions a rug in a rich person's house, it's always called Persian. I looked up the price out of curiosity and almost had a heart attack. A Persian rug can cost up to three hundred thousand dollars.

However, despite the whole house being beautiful, it's the kitchen that enchants me. It's what I would call paradise. Maybe because she owns a restaurant, Orla has turned this space into heaven for anyone who, like me, loves cooking. I could easily spend days in here without getting bored, and when I told her this, she laughed.

Gradually, I start to feel comfortable in her presence. Like Cillian, she is not disingenuous, and can sometimes be a bit rude. In any case, I prefer people like that to those who pretend to be perfect and are actually monsters, like my mother was.

As I play with the fork over the frosting of the cupcake I brought for dessert, I feel everyone's eyes on me, but it's Cillian's that make me the most uneasy.

He doesn't hide that he's studying every little action of mine, which makes me tremble and anxious.

The others asked subtle questions about my present and past, but when their cousin, Lorcan, spoke to me, I felt like I was in an interrogation room.

Not that he was rude or anything. I mean, all four are rough, but not rude. What I'm trying to say is that it seemed like the man was following a mental script of what he wanted to find out.

I answered most of the questions. As for others, those that came too close to my nightmare, I played dumb, as if I didn't understand, and sidestepped. I have the feeling he noticed but let it slide.

I keep my head down and hear Orla occasionally scolding her "boys." Each of them has already had at least four *cupcakes*. She wasn't kidding when she said they loved sweets.

It's funny that they respect her so much, even though they are all grown men. It's somewhat like my cousins with Aunt Eimear.

"I'd like to use the restroom," I say. "Where is it?"

Before anyone can answer, Cillian gets up.

"Come on. I'll take you."

I'm not usually easily embarrassed, but the fact that the whole family is watching us makes me want to run away.

I get up, completely focused on not falling, because my legs feel like jelly. Everything I've avoided while being here is about to happen: being alone with the man who drives my body wild.

Chapter 19

Cillian

My body reacts violently to her proximity.

I have every reason to keep my distance, especially now that I know a little more about her past, but as Juno walks down the long hallway on the lower floor of my aunt's house, the desire to pull her to me, to taste that sweet mouth again, is almost visceral.

She keeps her head down as she walks, and I wish I could guess what she's thinking. I've watched my brothers and especially Lorcan question her indirectly for over two hours.

Did she notice? I think so, because some of her answers were nothing more than evasive.

As she walks, one foot in front of the other, as if making an effort to keep her balance, I can't take my eyes off the gentle sway of her hips.

I'm not the poetic or romantic type, but everything about the woman makes me want to worship every inch of her body.

I remember what I found out a few days ago, and my fists clench at my sides.

We don't know much more than what Rick told us before he died, but as sure as the sunrise, I will find out if any of Doireann's lovers are still alive. If so, they'll wish they weren't.

We reach the bathroom door and Juno doesn't notice. I think she's so nervous that instead of letting me lead, she walked as if she were guiding me.

Before she can walk away further, I grab her by the arm.

Her flesh burns in my fingers and I should just point her to the bathroom as originally planned, but instead, I pull her closer.

She's not short, and her body is full of curves, but compared to me, she seems small and delicate, fitting perfectly into my embrace.

"Did I pass it?"

She breathes heavily and tries to hide her nervousness.

I don't answer. I tilt her chin up.

She looks at me and in the strangest and most fucked-up way, I realize she knows exactly who I am. I can see in her eyes that she sees my darkness, but there's no trace of fear in her perfect face.

Her hands flatten against my chest and I want to order her to touch me properly. I want to tell her to open my shirt so I can feel her delicate fingertips against me.

"Why don't you look at me?"

"Because I don't know how to act. As I told you on the phone, I got the message. I'm the obligation you feel attracted to."

"You're not just that."

"What am I then, Cillian? Do I have a name in your life? The little girl you protected, keeping her alive outside the country?"

I open the bathroom door and pull her inside. I lock it and lean against it.

"You are that too, but not just that."

"What then?"

"I'm not a good guy, but I feel like a pervert wanting you. That's not why I kept you safe."

"You only saw me once, when I was almost a teenager. We never had any connection beyond the short phone calls you made. — I can see you're angry, but you're also being honest, exposing yourself, and it turns me on like crazy. — Anyway, you made your point that day, at my house. Have sex and move on."

I don't deny it, because what she said is nothing but the truth.

Juno closes her eyes as if trying to calm herself; I can almost feel how fast her heart is racing.

When she opens them again, I realize too late that Juno is as dangerous to me as I am to her. The girl looks at me as if she can see all my past and present sins and still says: I'm still here.

Her cheeks are flushed with excitement, no doubt, but also with her combative side. The intensity of her reactions to me makes me want her with more fervor.

"And that's not what you want, I assume: sex without strings attached."

I say this more to provoke her, because deep down I know, even without having tasted her yet, that a few nights with Juno won't be enough. There's a warning inside me that says the moment I lose myself inside her body, I won't stop anytime soon.

She doesn't respond, but her chest rises and falls rapidly, showing that I'm not the only one crazy with desire.

I take her wrist and slowly rub my thumb over it, then bring it to my mouth. I run my tongue and teeth over the sensitive flesh, and when she shudders and moans softly, I forget where we are.

Having Juno in my arms is like watching light fade into darkness, and if I were a good man, I would let her go, but that's not what I'm going to do.

"I want you," I say, pinning her against the door.

My mouth hides in the curve where her neck meets her shoulder. I want to bite her, suck that piece of flesh, and hear her scream my name.

At this moment, there's no past or any bond between us other than a male's desire for his female.

She doesn't push me away, doesn't refuse me, doesn't tell me to stop. These would be expected reactions, especially since I haven't hidden who I am, but Juno doesn't do any of that.

Despite all the arrogance in her personality, there's so much innocence in her that I almost wish she would push me away.

She doesn't, and my hold on her body tightens.

"Say you don't want me," I command.

"How could I? That would be a lie."

"Christ, Juno."

I grab her neck, taking her mouth for myself. The meeting of our lips in this second kiss is anything but gentle. It's raw surrender. Unmasked seduction. Angry desire, because it shouldn't exist.

We know we're not right for each other and yet, we can't avoid the hunger we feel.

The uncontrollable effect she has on me makes my pressure against her body and the taking of her lips almost cruel.

Juno opens her mouth, and my tongue invades, demanding her surrender, showing her that I will accept nothing less than total domination over her.

I kiss her deeply. Fiercely, crazed with desire, almost punishing her for being so delicious.

She grips my hair tightly, as if wanting to take a part of me, as if warning that she will want more than I've given anyone else until now.

She grinds her tempting body against mine and I roar into her mouth with that display of hot passion.

"You don't know what you're getting into," I warn.

"I didn't say I agreed with anything," she says, breathless. "It was just a kiss."

At the same time she says that, her body undulates, molding itself, inviting.

I spin her around, facing her towards the door. I push her long hair aside and bite her ear while pressing my arousal against her ass, right where her panties are buried.

She moans and, as if unable to control her own body, she grinds.

"You're mine, Juno. We didn't know that when fate put you in my path, but you've always been mine."

Chapter 20

Cillian

Even savoring every second, she still refuses to accept my demand.

"Until you get tired? No, thanks. It's not my plan to be just another on the Boss's list."

"You lie so poorly. We both know that if I lifted this dress now, I'd find you wet. You might be inexperienced, but I have no doubt that you've already pleasured yourself. There's too much fire in you to have never even tried."

She turns her face, bringing her mouth close to mine but not touching.

"Once, but I couldn't make myself come."

Damn.

My breathing is erratic as my hands now roam her bare thighs, lifting her dress. I hold the sides of her lingerie, and she becomes so rigid that I stop kissing her, giving her a chance to interrupt me.

She doesn't ask me to stop; instead, she rubs her cheek against my mouth and sticks out her ass. My self-control is going to hell.

"Spread your thighs."

It's a test. I'm crazed with desire, but I'm not an animal. I want her to know where we're headed.

She does as I command without hesitation. The woman seems to know how to drive me insane. The submission she gives me with her body, contrary to what her mouth says, turns her into the most delicious contradiction.

Before I can touch her, however, a knock on the door interrupts us, and then I hear my cousin's voice.

"Aunt Orla wants to know if you two are alive."

Fuck me! Damn. I must be losing my mind.

I was about to make the girl come for the first time in Orla's bathroom.

"We're coming out," I say.

"Oh my God. Everyone will know that the two of us, that I and you..."

I pull down her dress and spin her around, making her face me.

"And what if they do?"

"What do you mean, 'and what if'? Orla is your aunt, and I like her. She won't want me here anymore if she knows I..."

"That you what? Took advantage of my body?"

Her face turns even redder and then, angry.

"You're mocking me," she accuses.

"We're adults, Juno. I admit I shouldn't have attacked you like this in my aunt's house, but you're delicious."

She seems to be struggling with herself, and I feel like an ass. It wasn't my intention to embarrass her in Orla's house.

"You have the same effect on me," she says, looking down. "I'd never let another person go this far."

Her skin is still warm, and I can smell her arousal.

Her blue eyes seem to be in a storm, but at the moment I'm not focused on that, but on what she said.

Never let another person go this far.

Almost an echo of what Orla said at the restaurant.

Another.

Even if I seduce her, there will be another for her. Or others. Juno is beautiful and young.

"I think we better leave, but you go first. I still need to use the bathroom," she says.

She says this casually, as if just a few minutes ago I wasn't about to give her her first orgasm.

Her self-control, so superior to mine at the moment, for some unknown reason, drives me insane. And then, I cross the line and say something that will change everything between us:

"Soon, we'll finish what we started today. When you come for the first time, it will be in my mouth."

I give her a light kiss on the lips and am satisfied when the pose of indifference falls away.

I move her out of my way so I can leave the bathroom before I end up fulfilling the promise right then and there.

"I DON'T WANT TO GET involved," Lorcan says, standing in the hallway.

"But you're going to do it anyway."

He shrugs.

"I'm just stating the obvious: despite being born into our world, the girl is as sweet as the cupcakes she makes. Knowing what you now know about her past, do you really want to go down this path?"

"What does that mean?"

"I'm not a psychologist or anything close to it, but we don't know the damage that's been done inside her, Cillian. In fact, even you, who have protected her for so many years, don't know much about her. But I think there's something pretty obvious to anyone who was at that table during lunch: Juno isn't the type of woman you can play with. She trusts you. Don't use that as a weapon to seduce her."

"You don't know what you're talking about."

"Maybe not. As I said before, I don't want to get involved."

Juno opens the bathroom door and looks from one to the other, seemingly sure we're talking about her. Despite that, she doesn't say anything. I can see she's embarrassed by Lorcan because she knows he caught us, but still, she raises her chin and walks past us without making any comments.

"That's not the only reason you came to talk to me now. What happened?"

"My grandfather is in Boston."

"And why should I care?"

"He wants to negotiate mutual protection for the routes in the center of the country."

"Why?"

"The Mexicans are causing problems."

"Tell me something new."

"No. This time it's serious. Los Morales are out of control. They're completely suicidal. If a war against the Russians starts, we'll have to take a side."

"And you're suggesting I ally with Yerik? No way."

"This has nothing to do with him being my cousin, Cillian, but because if the FBI starts a witch hunt, all the organizations will be brought into it."

"We can take care of our own asses, Lorcan. I don't want any kind of deal with the Russians."

"At least listen to what my grandfather has to say."

I run my hands over my face, incredibly frustrated.

"When?"

"Tomorrow."

"As long as it's somewhere where we won't be seen together."

"I'll arrange it at my apartment. Neutral enough for you?"

"I'll give half an hour of my time out of respect for your grandfather, Lorcan, and not because he's an ex-Pakhan."

"It doesn't matter the reason, as long as we can get rid of those fucking Morales."

"If shit hits the fan, you'll have to pick a side, cousin. You can't serve both God and the Devil."

He smiles.

"In that case, it would be serving the Devil and Satan. You know there's no choice to be made, Cillian. I'm your blood. I'll die for you."

"Then why the hell should I meet with Ruslan?"

"Because he's my grandfather. My blood too."

"Does Yerik know about this?"

"If I had to guess, not at the moment, but he'll eventually find out."

Chapter 21

Juno

I pretend once again not to notice everyone staring at me. The only one who hides it a bit better is Orla, who serves coffee and tea as if I hadn't spent almost ten minutes with her nephew in her bathroom.

However, when I lift my head and focus on one of Cillian's brothers, I notice something strange in their gazes.

It's as if they're trying to decipher me.

"When do you plan to open the shop, Juno?" It's Mad Lion asking, and not for a moment do I doubt that everyone present already knows about my plans for the future.

Cillian and his cousin haven't returned yet, and I wonder if they're talking about me.

God, what was I thinking letting the man kiss me like that, especially in his aunt's bathroom? If Lorcan hadn't interrupted us, I don't even know what might have happened. How embarrassing!

"We're going out on Tuesday to secure the property. After that, I'll find someone to do the necessary work and adjustments so we can open the shop soon," Orla responds in my place. "Juno is in her final period, and I'm sure she'll manage to balance her studies and work."

"Do you really think so?" I ask, for the first time letting my guard down in front of everyone.

I don't usually let people see my insecurities, but there's something about this family that makes me feel relaxed enough to show some of my fears.

"If I didn't think so, I wouldn't suggest you start your business now," their aunt replies, with her characteristic directness.

Cillian returns to the room with Lorcan and catches the end of the conversation.

"You'll have all the support you need to start your business. There's nothing to worry about."

His tone has shifted from the sensual command he used when touching my body a few minutes ago to speaking as if he were talking to a child, which annoys me.

Just as I can't understand what he makes me feel, Cillian also has no idea what I am to him now.

"I loved the lunch, Mrs. Orla..." I start, but she interrupts me:

"Orla, just," the hostess says. "We've talked about this."

"Alright. Orla. But it's time to go."

"If your concern is having clients, you already have four guaranteed here," Kellan says, returning to the subject of the bakery.

"Five," their aunt adds. "Besides, I'll want the cupcakes to serve at my restaurant, at brunch, on Sundays."

I was almost getting up, but I sit back down. I researched her restaurant online. It's huge.

"Are you serious?"

She gives a rare smile.

"I'm always serious when it comes to business, Juno. I have no doubt that your sweets will be a success."

I try to hide how much her praise warms me inside, but I think I fail because the guys start laughing.

"Jesus, I didn't even know there were women who blushed anymore," Kellan says. "I could fall in love with you just for that, Juno."

Something makes me turn not to him, but to Cillian, who at this moment is giving his brother a cold stare.

Now everyone else joins the middle O'Callaghan in laughter, and I feel like I'm on the outside, in some sort of private game between them.

"Come on, I'll take you home," Cillian says, and before I can think about what I'm doing, I get up.

There's something about the man that makes me obey his command, as if my body wants to submit even before my mind decides to.

Orla comes to say goodbye to me, and then to her nephew. After that, I give a "goodbye" from afar to the guys.

Cillian, like the day we left the building where the fights take place, puts his hand on the small of my back and guides me out of the house.

I shiver at his touch simply because I can't help it. I wish I were more experienced and could act indifferent to him.

As he opens the door for me to get into his car, I wonder if he's aware of the effect he has on me, but then I feel like giving myself a slap on the forehead.

Of course he is, you fool. You practically handed everything to him on a silver platter when you confessed how he makes you feel.

He settles behind the wheel, and through the side mirror, I see two cars preparing to leave as well. I know they're the bodyguards. Even my father, who I don't think was that important within the Syndicate, never left alone, as far as I remember. There was always at least one man with him.

"No driver today?"

"I dismissed him after I found out you were here."

My pulse quickens, and I can't help but ask:

"Why?"

"We need to talk."

Something in his tone makes me realize that I'm not going to like the content of this conversation.

"About the bakery?" I ask, even though I already know it has nothing to do with that.

"No."

He doesn't add anything else, watching as I fasten my seatbelt.

When I finish, he seems satisfied and puts both hands on the steering wheel.

The tattoo of a dragon on the back of his right hand, which I had noticed since the first time we met, catches my attention again.

"Is that why they call you Dragon?"

He turns his gaze back to me.

"What?"

"The tattoo on your hand."

"My mother loved the Chinese horoscope and called me Dragon since I was a child, because it's my sign. Even though I hated it, the nickname caught on and everyone started calling me that. When she died, I got the tattoo in her honor."

He says all this while gripping the steering wheel tightly, and I wonder if it's because that conversation makes him remember the loss of his parents.

At the same time that I'm sure Cillian is tough and cold, he isn't a monster in everything, because he was able to mark his skin in such an obvious and visible place, even hating the nickname, to honor his mother.

He doesn't seem happy to have confessed that to me, so trying to ease his frown, I reveal:

"My father also believed in the Chinese horoscope. I'm a tiger. He gave me a bracelet with a silver pendant of that animal. I still have it, even though I don't wear it anymore."

"I know."

"How is that possible?"

"I know everything about you, Juno. There are very few things I don't know, in fact, but let's clarify what's left today."

My heart sinks with the certainty of what I had already suspected: he wants to talk about the past.

Chapter 22

Cillian

"Are you coming up?" she asks as I park in her garage.

"I'm not going to attack you if that's what you're thinking," I say, because somehow, the fear she shows makes me feel like shit.

"I'm not afraid of being alone with you," she says, as if she could read my thoughts, "but because I know you're going to want to talk about things I don't like to remember."

"I need to know everything."

She looks at me for a moment before getting out of the car.

Half of my bodyguards go ahead to check her apartment, and Juno doesn't ask how they'll get in. She probably knows that, like me, they have the code that gives them access to her place.

Less than five minutes later, they return, saying everything has been properly inspected.

"Wait for me here," I say, making it clear that they won't be coming up in the elevator with us, but I know they'll go up the stairs and position themselves there.

In my world, following rules means ensuring I'll be alive the next day.

She doesn't say anything or even look at me when we enter the elevator.

"I'm not doing this to hurt you."

"Then why? Why make me remember that?"

"To punish anyone who's touched you, in whatever way."

The elevator stops, and she goes to the panel to enter the apartment code.

I let her go in first, and after she passes, I lock the door and lean against it.

"I'll try to make it as painless as possible."

Juno was walking to the living room but stops and looks back at me, angry.

"I thought pain was your specialty."

Even though she's trying to show courage, I can now see her a bit better. Behind the anger, she's suffering.

"You need to stop pretending just once and tell me the truth, Juno."

"Pretending? I've never pretended."

"You haven't been honest with me all these years."

"You never asked me the truth, Cillian. You assumed that your friend was the perfect mother and took care of me as a way to honor her. And I didn't even know it was because of her that you did what you did."

"I failed you by not staying closer."

"No. I didn't need you. What you gave me was enough."

I don't argue. She has the right to be angry.

"Tell me what happened the day your parents died, Juno."

She turns her back to me and walks to the window.

"You said you didn't want to hurt me, but the moment I let the memories come back, they will make me suffer."

I follow her.

"I know, but it will exorcise you too. Have you talked about the past with anyone?"

"Aunt Eimear knows."

I stop beside her, but she doesn't look at me. Her eyes seem lost in the street below us.

"How much do you know?" she asks.

"Based on what you had told me, I went looking. I found out many things, but not everything."

"Wait here a moment? I'm going to change."

Less than ten minutes pass before she comes back. She's now wearing denim shorts and a sleeveless top.

She chooses an armchair to sit in, and I understand that she needs to keep her distance.

She pulls her legs up to her body, hugging them as if trying to protect herself.

"You said Doireann was your friend for a few years. I believe it. She was a fraud." Her words come out flat, devoid of emotion. "But she was never a mother to me. She pretended when I was very little, I think to deceive my father, and even back then, she didn't mistreat me. She was just indifferent, I think. I don't remember her being affectionate with me."

"What changed?"

She shrugs.

"I don't know. I think it was less than a year before they died because I was ten, almost eleven. They were never in love, but my dad did everything she wanted, which seemed to make her happy. Suddenly, the fights started. I'm not sure what happened, I've tried to remember, but I can't recall the details, except that it was around their wedding anniversary celebration."

I feel the weight of a heavy metal ball in my stomach, the intuition about what triggered the tragedy confirming itself.

Grady, Juno's father, invited me to their wedding anniversary, and I normally wouldn't have gone, but since I hadn't seen Doireann for over a decade and for the sake of how close we were in the past, I decided to attend.

"Continue."

"She came back different. She was never a loving mother like Dad was, but from that day on, she became cruel. It was a shock at first. I had never been hit, and suddenly she was attacking me for no reason."

"And your dad, where was he?"

"Traveling, most of the time. I'm not sure what he did for the *Syndicate*.

Her eyes meet mine but quickly look away. It's the first time Juno openly talks about her knowledge of what I do.

"Why didn't you tell him?"

"Because she begged me. After she would hit me, she'd cry in regret and say that if Dad found out she'd 'lost control,' he would leave with me and our family would be torn apart. I never had a perfect family, but it was still a family. My safety."

I nod, agreeing, keeping my rage against Doireann under control as best I can.

"Continue."

"After a few weeks, men started coming to our house. Some, I remembered seeing with my dad, but most, I didn't know. She and her 'partners' did things in my parents' room." Juno shakes her head from side to side, her face showing disgust. "Even though I was still young, I knew it was wrong and told her, after one of them left, that I would tell my dad. She swore no one would come to our house again, and once again, stupidly, I forgave her."

"You wanted your whole family. There's nothing wrong with that."

"I also betrayed my dad, Cillian. Somehow, I helped her deceive him."

I see the guilt on her face and know there's no comfort for that.

It's fucked up that even now she carries that weight, but no words in the world will rid her of the remorse.

"Your mother was good at pretending. I met her and never imagined she was capable of such things."

She nods.

"Unfortunately for me, not telling my dad the truth wasn't just a betrayal, it was my greatest mistake too. I didn't know yet, but my nightmare was just beginning."

Chapter 23

Cillian

"That day, my father came home and I kept the promise I made to my mother. I didn't tell him anything. I only found out the next morning that he would be away for months."

"I sent him to the west coast," I say more to myself than to her.

It was one of the things that intrigued me about that tragedy. Because on the very day he came back home, after traveling for so long, Grady could have taken such drastic action.

If there had been evidence of infidelity, I would understand, but I know that wasn't the case. There was a man waiting outside for him because he still had work to do that night. He told me that between Grady arriving and hearing the shots, no more than half an hour passed.

When I asked him if he knew why all that shit happened, he said there were rumors that Doireann had a lover.

A lover.

It's not a fucking commendable thing for a married woman, but I thought she was lonely, frustrated, and it was just a slip-up. I believed that Grady lost control when he could have chosen divorce, but now that I know much of Juno's nightmare, I understand that he did what he did in the heat of the moment, or he would never have left his girl orphaned. With the knowledge and special skills to make bodies disappear, he could have gotten rid of Doireann without anyone ever finding a clue.

"From the day my father left, she started bringing men there daily. She also started drinking more and hitting me too. I said I would tell the teacher, so she stopped sending me to school. One day, one of her men accidentally came into my room. I screamed, terrified, and told him to leave. My mother came in and laughed. She ordered the man to hit me to discipline me, and that's how it all started."

I stand up, unable to listen to that while sitting still. A familiar desire for death coursing through my body.

"I'd kill her myself now if your father hadn't done it." She looks at me, eyes wide, but I don't back down. "I'd love to squeeze her neck, watch her die."

My voice sounds unchanged. Killing is as routine to me as eating. I wouldn't lose a night's sleep over punishing that bitch. When I think of Doireann now, she's no longer the friend from adolescence but the one who hurt my Juno.

Yes, *mine*, even if she'll hate me when she discovers my role in all this.

"Tell me the rest."

"The men started coming more than once a day. Sometimes I managed to hide, other times, there was no time."

My fist clenches.

"Hide?"

"There was a hole in my closet. I think she didn't know, but my dad did. He wanted to fix it, but I asked him not to. I liked to take a flashlight in there and read. Especially after my mother's lovers started coming."

She says each word as if talking about a third person, not her own childhood. Despite that, her lower lip trembles and her voice sounds dragged.

"When I heard the front door open, I would hide and they couldn't find me, but one day she discovered my hiding place. She didn't even ask one of her boyfriends to hit me; she beat me herself. The next day, she made me drink juice with a strange taste. I felt like throwing up and slept all day."

"Was that the first time?"

"Yes."

"Alright. What else?"

"The second time she made me drink the juice, not to make her angrier, I pretended to drink it. I think I miscalculated because I ended up swallowing it anyway and got dizzy, but not as much as she thought. Doireann kept asking if I was sleepy and I said yes because she would go crazy when contradicted, and at that point, I knew it was best not to upset her. I pretended to sleep, but I think I actually dozed off at some point. I woke up with a man touching my underwear. My mother was also in the room. I was terrified. I wasn't wearing shorts anymore and knew I hadn't taken off my own clothes. I was eleven and understood that it was wrong. My dad had explained to me never to let a man touch me."

I punch the wall, bile rising in my throat.

Juno's eyes are filled with tears.

"I screamed and fought. I think I caught them both by surprise. I locked myself in the room and then went into the hiding place. She banged on the door, made threats. I didn't open. Soon after, I heard the phone ring. Looking back now, I think it was my dad who called. Probably saying he was coming back because suddenly, everything went silent."

"She didn't try to get back into the room?"

"Yes. And she made promises too. Tried to trick me again with her lying words. I didn't believe her. I hated her and wanted Dad to come and hurt her like she did to me."

She is crying a lot now, her words coming out with difficulty.

"Juno..." I take a step closer, but she stops me with a hand gesture.

"Let me finish. I thought it was my lucky day when, a while later, I heard the door open and then my dad's voice. I came out of hiding.

I ran to him. Doireann came after us. She tried to lead him to their room, but when Dad picked me up, he didn't let me go. He smelled the alcohol on me and asked what it was. I started crying and my mom, as always, lied. Said I drank secretly. Dad didn't believe her. He kicked her out of my room and demanded to know what happened. I told him everything. About the men hitting me and what happened that day. I wanted him to know I fought back. He said I was his little tigress, like the charm on the bracelet he gave me, and I wanted to prove it was true."

I can't keep my distance any longer. I reach her in the armchair and sit with her on my lap.

"Enough. I already understand."

Fuck! I wasn't prepared for the impact her suffering had on me. I thought I'd never feel anything like what I experienced the day my parents died, but imagining her at the mercy of that fucked-up sicko drives me crazy.

"No. Let me talk. I don't want to think about this after today."

I don't think it will be possible. Whatever way this story ends, Juno will carry it for the rest of her life and it only makes me hate her mother even more.

"When I finished telling him everything, something happened that I had never seen before. My dad cried. It wasn't a cry of pain, but of anger, and I think desperation too. I knew what anger felt like because I felt it towards my mother every day. He then hugged me and kissed my forehead. Then, he laid me on the bed and told me not to leave the room. Not even a minute passed before I heard a loud noise. Dad had taken me hunting in Montana once, and I knew the sound of gunfire. I ran to the door, but before I got there, there was another shot. I was afraid Doireann had hurt him. I wasn't afraid for myself. I wanted to save him. When I got to the living room, she was lying in her own blood. He was too, but still alive, and he asked for my forgiveness. He said he had failed me. I never had the chance to tell him he was wrong. I was the one who failed my dad. By telling the truth, I killed him."

Chapter 24

Juno

I'm not good at accepting comfort. Not even my aunt could manage that for me. The only time I opened up to her, and not with as many details as I did with Cillian, she tried to hug me, but I didn't want it.

Being comforted prevents me from pretending it doesn't hurt as much.

However, when he pulled me into his lap, holding me in his arms, I didn't want to leave; I wanted to stop hiding. I don't want to make a habit of it, but just for today, I'll allow myself to be held and cared for.

He doesn't say anything more. He doesn't comfort me with empty words or say that my father's death wasn't my fault.

I respect him a little more for that. Few people understand that words cannot make the pain go away.

I don't know how long I cry. Cillian doesn't run his hand through my hair or make any noise.

He simply does what I need: holds me in the protective wall of his arms. He hugs me like I've never been hugged before. Silently promises that with him, I will always be safe.

"I'm not a victim," I say after a while, but without looking at him.

"I never said you were."

"But you thought it. I've never talked to anyone besides you and my aunt about this, but I did some research. People like Doireann only do what they do to the defenseless. I was a child and couldn't defend myself. Today, the story would be different."

"Today, you are under my protection. You will never have to dirty your hands."

"Under your control, you mean."

"Also. Anyway, no matter what label you give it, you are safe."

"I don't want to go around killing people, but I need to learn to defend myself."

"We can talk about that another time, Juno. It's too much for just one day."

I turn around in his lap.

"Just don't pity me. Don't change towards me after what I told you."

"I don't pity you. That's an unworthy feeling. I feel hatred, maybe a bit beyond the hatred for those who hurt you. And more than anything, I feel guilty."

I stiffen in his lap, and when I try to get up, he doesn't stop me.

"Guilty?" I repeat, feeling my stomach churn. I look at him more closely, studying his body and face. "What are you talking about?"

He stands up as well, and I think he knows what's going through my mind.

"I was never at your house, if that's what you're thinking. I'm a monster, not a pedophile or child beater."

I feel ashamed of myself because I know he's speaking the truth.

"I'm sure you were never there. I remember every face."

His expression clears up a bit.

"Even the day she got you drunk?"

"Not the first time, as I said before. But I'll never forget the man who touched me."

"I need you to look at some photographs of members of the *Syndicate*. I want you to see if you recognize anyone."

"Alright, but first tell me why you said you feel guilty."

"You told me your mother changed after their wedding anniversary. I might have been the cause of that change."

"What? How?" I walk to the other side of the room. "You and her... you..."

"No, I never touched her like I would touch a woman." He sits down, his elbows resting on his knees, and even in a pose that shows exhaustion, he seems intimidating.

"Then I don't understand."

"Do you know how your parents met?"

"In Ireland. I think when they fell in love, Dad was visiting my grandfather's country... my country too, I mean, since I'm half Irish. Or rather, when he fell in love with her, because knowing what I know about Doireann now, I don't think she ever loved anyone."

"And what else do you know?"

"About our family? Not much. Dad was born here but was the son of an American. Half Irish, only."

"That's right. Like most of us. When your father and mother got together, I was living here. I was my uncle's right-hand man, but too young to be the boss. Years later, my uncle died, but before that, he passed control of the *Syndicate* to me."

"What does that have to do with my parents?"

"Long before I moved permanently to the United States, your mother and I were friends. Neighbors. She stood by me when my parents were murdered. To me, she was never more than a sister, but after a while, I realized she wanted more. I didn't even need to bother clarifying that there would never be a romance between us because shortly after, I was called to come live here. Maybe it was a mistake not to tell her openly that I didn't feel anything for her as a woman."

"But you gave her hope?"

"When I was younger, I was exactly what I am now, Juno. I only do what I want. I only stay with who I want. I don't deal in half-measures. Either I desire a woman or I don't. I wasn't interested in Doireann that way."

"Right. Sorry for interrupting you."

"Your mother and I lost touch. After a while, I learned she was getting married. I thought she had really fallen for your father. I didn't attend the ceremony, but as I do with everything in my life, I kept informed from a distance and was satisfied to see that everything seemed to be going well between them. On their wedding anniversary — he runs his hand through his hair — the one you referred to when the changes began... I hadn't seen her in many years, and I thought that after all that time, married and a mother, Doireann would know that all there could ever be between us was friendship."

"But that wasn't what she wanted."

"No. She got drunk and followed me into the bathroom. She offered herself. — He closes his eyes for a moment. — She *showed* herself, practically naked, and I said no. She asked if it was because of her. It wasn't. I didn't want her, never wanted her, but there was no reason to hurt her for nothing. In the name of the past, I told her that she was a woman with a family and should act accordingly. It didn't help. She screamed and said that if you didn't exist, I would want her, that I always wanted her. I blamed much of what happened on the alcohol she had consumed."

Nothing he says surprises me.

"What happened next?" I ask.

"Your father showed up. I told him to take her home."

"Why did you say it was your fault?"

"The betrayals. Not accepting her own life. I was the one who triggered that. She told me she would be the perfect woman for me, that she wanted to rule by my side. To be the First Lady of the *Syndicate*."

I get up and kneel in front of him.

"Do you think she did what she did because she was in love with you? She wasn't, Cillian. Doireann never loved anyone."

"I believe it, but in her disturbed mind, she might have thought so. Anyway, I contributed to destroying her life, Juno. Even before knowing your whole story, I thought that night had been the trigger for Doireann to betray your father, but I had no idea of the damage I caused along the way. I was never your savior; I was the cause of your nightmare."

"No. My mother was a monster, Cillian."

He stands up.

"And you think I'm what? Some fucking saint? Don't kid yourself, Juno. I'm just a monster of a different kind, but still, a monster."

Chapter 25

Cillian

"You're not like her."

"Because I would never hurt my own blood, but that doesn't mean I wouldn't harm other people's children."

"Children?" she asks, horrified.

"No. I've never hurt children or ordered anyone to do so, but killing is part of my job, and you know that."

Before she can respond, my phone rings.

The words Lorcan says open the gates of hatred that I've barely managed to control during this entire conversation.

"*We found another one.*"

I get up and start walking toward the door.

"Where are you going?"

"To do what I do best: punish."

She doesn't ask me anything because despite everything, Juno understands how things work in my world.

I close the door as I leave.

My head is boiling. Feelings and emotions I've never experienced before.

I've never felt another's pain.

When my parents died, I mourned for myself. For never being able to have them by my side again. For them never having the chance to meet future grandchildren.

I went hunting for the men who killed them and those who ordered their deaths. I tortured them, executed them, and celebrated watching the life drain from their worthless bodies, all to satisfy my thirst for blood. For revenge, because I don't know the concept of forgiveness.

Today, for the first time, I felt pain outside of myself. Her pain.

I wanted the power to go back in time and erase her past. To have seen who Doireann was and to have killed her before she had spread her trail of destruction in the innocent daughter's life.

I enter the garage and tell one of my men to take my car back home. Then, I tell them where we need to go. It's outside Boston. About forty kilometers, but I'm not in a hurry. Tonight will be long.

It will take a long time before I can purge all my hatred.

I GET OUT OF THE VEHICLE and head towards the abandoned warehouse. This place is not like the basement of the fight building. Only special guests are brought here, and Lorcan knows exactly what I will need tonight.

If I gave Rick a quick death for not yet understanding the extent of what Juno had been through, tonight, after seeing her pain, my new guest won't be so lucky.

As soon as I enter the place, Lorcan comes to meet me. My brothers are here as well.

"Get out."

"We'll wait for you outside," Odhran says.

"It won't be quick."

"We're not in a hurry."

"Did you interrogate him?"

"Yes. We didn't discover anything beyond what we learned from Rick. That son of a bitch... huh... beat her. Nothing more."

"I know," I say.

"You know? How?"

"Aside from Doireann's attempt to have Rick abuse Juno, there was only one more. I need to be sure of who it is or if he's really dead. Juno told me she remembers the faces of all the men who were at her parents' house."

"We'll find them," Kellan says. "Even if we have to sit her down with a sketch artist. We'll track them down one by one."

"I specifically want the man who touched her. I'll give him special treatment."

They leave, and before I head to my guest, I go to a box where we keep our weapons. I know exactly what I want. Knives or revolvers won't be enough.

As I walk towards the man hanging from chains, I hear the scrape of my shoes on the floor. I slow my pace. No rush tonight.

Finally, after covering the hundred meters separating me from my subordinate, I reach him.

There are no initial words; I use my rage as fuel to hit him in both knees with the baseball bat. When the first cry of pain escapes his mouth, all I can think about is Juno, small, defenseless, and not understanding why she was subjected to such torture.

"Boss..."

"Do you know why you're going to die?"

"The girl," he says.

"Yes. She's no longer a girl now; she is much more of a woman than you will ever be a man."

"A quick death," he pleads.

"No. Your journey to hell will be long."

The next time I hit him, it's in the abdomen. I know exactly the points where the pain is most intense. I won't hit any vital organs, for now.

His screams don't tell me anything, as I can only remember the tears of my Juno earlier today.

I spend a lot of time beating him, but using only the exact pressure to cause suffering without hastening his death.

Eventually, the hatred finally subsides, and an intense cold replaces it. It's as if ice runs through my veins.

"You were my soldier. Not only did you betray a brother, but you abused his daughter."

"The woman... Doireann..." He can barely speak.

"Fuck what that bitch told you to do. You have a brain, damn it!"

"I would never... have touched her if I had known she would be yours."

"You should never have beaten any child, you fucked-up sicko."

I move closer, and he knows we're reaching the end. Until now, his face had only been worked over by the guys before I arrived because I saved him for last.

"I'm going to die... because of a cunt?"

I raise the bat and take my position. Almost in slow motion, I hear the air shift as I swing, and I savor every second as I watch his head disappear in a mass of blood.

"No. You died because I can't erase what was done to her, but I can honor her by punishing every son of a bitch who touched her."

I drop the bat on the ground and leave the warehouse.

There are splatters on my shirt, pants, and shoes. I strip off and my brother hands me clean clothes.

"Find them all," I order.

"Cillian," Lorcan calls to me, perhaps sensing my unstable state at the moment.

"Find the sketch artist. I want her to describe what she remembers about the man who touched her. When you find him, no one will lay a finger on him. That son of a bitch is mine."

I walk to my car, and as soon as I sit behind the wheel, my phone rings.

I squeeze my eyes shut for a moment, battling internally because I feel dirtier than ever, but I end up answering.

"Juno."

"I don't blame you. You might think you're the one to blame, but you're not. She was a monster and sooner or later, I think this would have happened."

"There's no way to be sure of that."

"No, there isn't, but I know it anyway. She didn't want us, either me or my father. Don't push me away because you feel guilty. Don't push me away for any reason."

She hangs up without saying goodbye and I know I've reached a crossroads.

Regardless of the past, the present is screaming, demanding a choice.

Chapter 26

Cillian

I didn't sleep, which isn't all that unusual. My head is always stuffed with problems, but last night, what became clear to me was the desire to go to her, even knowing it wasn't a good idea.

After all the revelations yesterday, I can't play with Juno like I have with other women.

"You don't want to play with her like you have with other women," a voice yells.

I jump out of the car in front of Lorcan's apartment, once again putting off the issue with Juno. Right now, I need to see what the *ex-Pakhan* wants with me.

As soon as I reach the lobby, my cousin calls me.

"He's already here."

"I know. There are at least half a dozen Russians thinking they're being discreet, hiding in cars on his street."

I take the stairs since his apartment is on the first floor. Just like Juno's, apart from Lorcan's two units, which he turned into a duplex, all the others belong to me.

When I reach his floor, my cousin is waiting for me outside.

"The situation is much worse than I thought."

"You're looking fucking agitated. What's up? Is it just the problem with the Mexicans that's got you like this?"

"There could be an unprecedented war if the *FBI* decides to come down on all the organizations. My grandfather is already thinking two steps ahead."

I shake my head, forcing a smile.

"I go crazy when I hear you call the *ex-Pakhan* Russian 'grandfather.' Fuck me, I like Ruslan, but not enough to have a common relative."

"Being a grandfather and father to so many people is part of the good times I had running around the world, my boy," the old man says, coming out into the hallway.

Yes, I know very well. Ruslan's sexual appetite is legendary. My father used to say that any attractive woman who passed in front of the Russian was immediately conquered.

"How are you, sir?"

"Getting by. Old age is a bitch. But aren't you coming in? As secure as this building is, what we need to discuss requires privacy."

Putting his arm over his grandson's shoulder, who is at least fifteen centimeters taller, the Russian heads back into the apartment.

We sit in the living room, and I see they're drinking beer.

Lorcan nods his head, offering me some, but I refuse.

"There's no comparison to how much better this beer is that you Irish make," he says, gesturing to a bottle of *Guinness Draught Stout*. "American beers taste like piss."

"I'm a whiskey man," I say.

"The best, I suppose? From that Scottish lad's distillery, Duke MacQuoid?"

"Yes. The man bottles liquid gold," Lorcan agrees. "This week alone, we received three cases of an excellent batch from his distillery."

"A few years ago, I was invited to an auction at the MacQuoid distillery," Ruslan says. "Rare vintage, bids starting at seven hundred thousand dollars. I won a case for a million."

"Fuck me!" My cousin shakes his head, and the grandfather laughs.

I stay quiet because if I mention that I bought a single bottle of sixty-year-old whiskey for a million and a half, Lorcan might have a heart attack.

The relaxed and unplanned conversation slowly makes me relax in the presence of the *ex-Pakhan*.

It's nothing against the man himself, but what he represents — the Russian mafia.

"I suppose we can deal with those fucking Mexicans now, right?" Ruslan asks.

"I'm listening," I respond in a neutral tone.

Regardless of my respect for the man, he needs to understand that this isn't a social gathering. The only reason we're talking is the blood tie that connects him to my cousin.

"Lorcan told you about *Los Morales*, right?"

"Yes, but I was already keeping an eye on their expansion from afar. They're ambitious, even invading other cartels' territories."

"And they're at open war with us," he says.

I stay silent because that isn't my problem, but rather Yerik's, the current Pakhan.

"I know what you're thinking, son. There's no need to get involved in a war that isn't yours, but I also know that you're starting out in the arms business."

"Which makes us your competitors."

"Not necessarily. We can negotiate routes. We've done that in the past."

"In exchange for what? Mutual protection?"

He takes a sip of his beer.

"No. We'd need protection if we wanted to keep them alive, which is not the case."

"They want to eliminate the entire cartel," Lorcan explains.

"They're weeds. They don't follow any rules," the Russian concludes.

I understand what he's saying. There's a greater risk for all organizations if one leaves traces. If the *FBI* picks up the trail, they'll come after all of us with their *dogs*, which will result in a bloodbath, multiple arrests, and worst of all, delays in the delivery of our goods.

"I suppose your *Pakhan* doesn't know about this proposal you're making me," I say to push him a bit because, in truth, I know that despite no longer being the leader of the Russian mafia, Ruslan still has a lot of influence in the Organization.

"No, not yet, but I still have autonomy within the Brotherhood to forge alliances," he says, as if reading my thoughts.

"Even with me?"

It's no secret how much Yerik and I loathe each other. Since I took power, the longest period without a dispute between us was after we both discovered we have Lorcan in common, although the Russian insists on pretending not to know my cousin.

"Even with you," he finally replies. "My grandson is as stubborn as I am, but he never lets emotions override the greater good, which is the safety of the Brotherhood."

"How long would this truce last? Until *Los Morales* are wiped out?" I ask.

"We don't even need to go that far. Just until they start to retreat. This war isn't yours, it's ours. Just make sure that when you encounter them along the way, you clean up."

"And what does the *Sindicato* gain in return?"

"As a gesture of good neighborliness, we'll clear two routes for your weapons."

I cross my arms, studying him. I know he's not telling the whole truth.

"That's not all. You've been at war before. There was never a need for a pact with us," I say.

"Besides the common interest in getting the *FBI* off our backs and ensuring that the goods move through your routes without external interference, what made me propose an agreement is that, like us, you understand the concept of family. The Mexicans don't. I have great-grandchildren now. Children who have nothing to do with our business. *Los Morales* don't care about that. To them, there's no distinction between women and children. If something happens to one of Yerik's children, the country will explode. My grandson won't leave a stone unturned. Everyone loses in the end, but my loss can never be recovered."

I stand up, signaling the end of the meeting.

"Talk to your *Pakhan*. If I get involved with you, I won't want just two routes, I want six. And with the guarantee that we won't suffer losses during the truce period. If a single box of weapons is lost, the deal is off."

"I'm going to Atlanta today. Tomorrow we'll have an answer."

I nod and open the door, but before I leave, he calls me:

"Cillian."

I turn back to face him.

"I know you're starting a personal hunt..."

I look at Lorcan, and he raises his arms in surrender.

"I didn't say anything."

"You didn't. Haven't you understood that I'm omnipresent? Very little happens on this planet that I don't know about. But I'm not here to brag, just to warn you to keep an eye on those closest to you. Maybe the person you're looking for is closer than you think."

Chapter 27

Juno

Almost a Week Later

"You're distracted," Orla accuses as we leave the *showroom*.

After choosing the store where my bakery will be set up, today was about selecting furniture. It's amazing how quickly things can happen when you have money to invest.

As promised, Cillian hired people to handle the administrative side: an accountant and a team to give me a basic understanding of sales, profits, and how to price my products.

Sometimes I feel a bit lost. There's so much information. In my naivety, I thought it would be enough to enter the kitchen and make my delicious pastries, but there's much more to running a food business than just cooking.

There are so many required licenses that I wonder how someone without all the support I'm getting manages.

Orla invited me to do a quick internship at her restaurant, since my classes don't start until the day after tomorrow, and I've been making the most of every bit of this hands-on learning.

I feel closer to her and yet, sometimes, I worry that I'm intruding on the O'Callaghan family's territory.

Cillian hasn't shown up since, although he messages me every day to see if I need anything. We've returned to the situation where he checks in on me from a distance.

I learned from Orla that he usually goes to the restaurant at least once a week for a meal with her, but he hasn't been there since I started interning with her.

"I was thinking that maybe I'm *overstepping* in your family."

"I don't understand," she says as we get into the car where the driver is waiting with the door open.

"You told me that Cillian used to visit your restaurant at least once a week, but he hasn't come since I started interning with you."

"Do you want me to tell you the rosy version of what I think about him keeping his distance, or the truth?"

I fasten my seatbelt and give a sad smile.

"My life has never had a rosy version."

I told her about my past. Everything, from the beginning, and also about the physical attraction between me and her nephew.

I spent years trying to forget my childhood, fleeing from memories, but since I spoke with him, it's become a bit easier to look back. It wasn't thinking about Doireann or what she did to me that prevented me from remembering, but the remorse I feel about my father's death.

I hope to one day forgive myself. For now, I haven't been able to.

The day before yesterday, Orla went with me to the cemetery to visit my father's grave. It was something I wanted to do since I arrived in Boston, but I lacked the courage.

I spent a long time talking to him, something I had already been doing in my prayers, but being there, in front of his gravestone, gave me a sense of closeness I had never felt before.

"Let us be alone for a few minutes," she says to the driver, and only after he leaves does she turn to me again. "My nephew is obsessed with punishing those who hurt you. He's on a hunt, and if I know him well, he won't be satisfied until he finds them."

Three days ago, Lorcan came to the restaurant and stayed with me and a sketch artist in Orla's office. Surprisingly, I didn't feel embarrassed that he also knew about my past. One thing I've learned about Cillian is that there's a very fine line between personal relationships and the *Sindicato*. Business mixes with family, and one's problem is everyone's problem.

Lorcan and the sketch artist wanted me to describe what I remembered about the men who used to visit my parents' house. Contrary to what I believed, after a decade, my memory played tricks on me.

Half an hour after talking to the man and trying to provide details about three different individuals, he told me I was mixing and repeating characteristics and that I should focus on one person at a time.

We agreed that I would try to focus on the one who haunted me the most: the man who was at my parents' house on the day of the tragedy. The monster who touched me.

"He never came to see me again," I say, returning to the present.

"Cillian works in a different way from the rest of us, Juno. He's not a man who does anything halfway. He resolves one issue and only then moves on to the next."

"Am I an *issue*?"

"I think, at the moment, he doesn't know how to classify you."

I look out the window.

"That's fine. Maybe it's better this way."

"My daughter, I love my nephew, but because I care about you so much too, I feel obligated to warn you."

I turn back to face her.

"Warn me?"

"Do you know who my husband was?"

I nod in agreement.

I know he was Cillian's father's older brother.

"The *ex-Boss*."

"Yes, he was in the position that Cillian holds now for over two decades. God didn't bless us with children, so my husband prepared his eldest nephew to be his successor. I lived within the *Sindicato* for all the years of our marriage. For better or for worse, I witnessed every war between the organizations, had to choke back tears many times seeing him come back wounded, stabbed."

I open my mouth to say that I also saw my father come back like that on some occasions, but she interrupts me:

"Back then, the wars between organizations were resolved almost like street fights: cars would explode, leaders would be eliminated. End of story. There was respect for family, though. Rarely did an organization go beyond its target. That has changed. Some of these gangs couldn't care less about limits or about killing children, for example."

"I don't understand. What does this have to do with Cillian and me?"

"I can't predict the future, but I can speak about what I observe. My nephew doesn't see you the same way he has dealt with other women in his life. Cillian isn't impulsive; everything he does is precise and calculated. He won't make a definitive move for you until he's sure of what he wants. However, the age difference between you is significant. You haven't experienced much yet, so I feel obligated to warn you: if you stay together, you won't be entering a fairy tale, Juno."

Chapter 28

Juno

Days Later

I walk outside of my college classroom after my third day of classes on American soil; I am increasingly happy to be nearing the end. As one of my cousins would say: when it begins, it's already ending.

Even in Dublin, I didn't enjoy the university environment much, maybe because I don't feel as young in my head as my biological age suggests.

How many of these people who smile, smoke, and treat college as a duty have had their parents die in front of them?

As soon as the self-pitying thought hits me, I get angry with myself for allowing myself to go down this path.

If I want to overcome what happened, it's not by comparing myself to happy families that I will succeed.

As I walk through the halls, some people greet or smile at me, and I return the gestures. I've noticed that other students talk to each other even without knowing each other, which is quite strange, but it must be some sort of rule of good social behavior—this kind of superficial friendship.

I'm finally outside the building and try to tell myself that my meeting with Cillian later will be like any other we've had, but the fluttering in my stomach betrays me because just the thought of seeing him again makes my heart race.

I listened carefully to everything Orla said to me on the day we chose the equipment and furniture for my shop, and after thinking about every word, I'm sure she was wrong.

Not about Cillian seeking revenge regarding my past. I believe that. However, I think his aunt is seeing much more than what exists between us. For a normal guy, I would already be a complication. Someone with too much baggage.

Why would a confirmed bachelor, who can have any woman he wants and much more, and who is the head of the Irish mafia, want something more from me than just sex?

I shake my head in anger at myself for returning to this question.

It has been upsetting feeling rejected by him, and since the day before yesterday, I decided that I won't spend my days waiting for him to make a move.

I don't need crumbs from anyone, not even from the only man who has ever made my heart race.

I was doing quite well with this determination until this morning when, during a class break, he called me saying he would meet me at my future shop because he wanted to see up close how the construction was going.

Even for me, who isn't the most confident person in the world, it sounded like an excuse to see me, but maybe it's just to check how I'm doing. Nothing more. He has never hidden that he is controlling and likes to have me under his domain.

The grand opening will be in three weeks, so there is also the possibility that he just wants to inspect how his money is being spent.

A cold breeze hits me, and I regret not bringing even a cardigan. I need to walk about half a kilometer between the building where I had class and the parking lot where my security is stationed. Even though we are barely speaking, the day before classes started, I sent Cillian a message asking him to keep his men there. I would feel ridiculous with someone following me into the college buildings. Besides, it would draw too much attention.

To my surprise, he agreed, as long as I didn't deviate from my path without informing them.

When he says things like that, I feel like a child, and it annoys me a lot.

I glance at the clock and see that it's almost five in the afternoon. At this hour, the *campus* is much emptier, with only small groups sitting on the grass.

I see some guys in tight t-shirts and jeans who don't look like students. They are tattooed, but not like my cousins or the other men from the *Sindicato* I've met. They have designs even on their faces.

No one needs to tell me that they mean trouble. Aunt Eimear was tired of chasing away some of her children's friends who seemed even more "misguided" than the men from the *Sindicato* I normally know. I learned to avoid these kinds of guys and to guard against danger.

I pass by them with my head down because my cousins taught me to never make eye contact with someone who makes me uncomfortable. Certain men interpret everything, even a mere glance, as an "invitation."

I'm sure they notice me when they start whistling and saying obscene words. I'm not a prude. I've heard some pretty nasty swear words from my cousins, but never directed at me. The things these men are saying make my stomach turn.

I start to sweat cold and quicken my pace. From where I am, I can already see the car with my security, but this time, unfortunately, they are not outside waiting for me.

My blood drains from my body when, unexpectedly, one of them positions himself beside me.

"Hey, didn't you hear me calling, princess?"

The man speaking to me has a heavy accent, and automatically, but without stopping, I look at him.

I step aside, not just because of the tattoos covering his face— it takes much more than a *bad boy* to scare me— but because of what I see in his eyes.

They are black, as if there were no iris. It's strange, and the first thing that comes to mind is that they resemble an abyss.

With my distance, he seems irritated and moves closer again.

I can see some of his friends walking up to where we are, and as fear starts to spread through my body, I try to convince myself that he won't do anything. It's broad daylight.

I almost run now, certain that it will be enough of a hint that I don't want to be bothered. However, I miscalculate the type of person I'm dealing with, as he grabs my arm.

It's a painful grip, and pain is something I don't handle well. It brings out the worst in me, reminding me of what I went through when I was defenseless.

Not anymore. I will never allow anyone to hurt me again.

Without stopping to think about anything other than getting rid of the hateful contact, with my free arm, I hit him in the face with all the force I have.

Perhaps caught off guard, he releases me.

I run away without looking back, but I can hear the laughter from the rest of the gang, as well as some curses directed at me.

Finally, one of the security guards seems to notice something is wrong and gets out of the car. I'm very close now, but before I can reach him, a hand grabs me by the shoulder.

I struggle, trying to get free, and end up bumping into the solid chest of my bodyguard's boss.

"Let her go," I hear Hingar growl.

The guy is still gripping my shoulder tightly, but Hingar wraps an arm around my waist, keeping me close. Finally, I'm free from his grip.

"You don't want to do this," the security guard continues in a cold tone.

When I turn around, still in his arms, I see that the guy who attacked me has a knife in his hands.

Some people approach, and his friends tell him to back off.

He puts away the weapon, and I don't take my eyes off his face, still terrified.

"One day we will meet again, princess. You can bet on that," he threatens before leaving.

Chapter 29

Juno

"This isn't the way to my apartment," I say when I see we're not taking the usual route.

I try to keep my voice neutral, but I'm still trembling a lot.

"We have orders from Cillian to take you to his place. You were supposed to meet the boss at your store, but after what we just reported, there's been a change of plans."

"Who were those guys, Hingar?" I ask.

I didn't expect him to answer, but I'm still irritated when he looks straight ahead again, as if I hadn't said anything.

I close my eyes, leaning back in the car seat, trying to understand what happened.

One minute I was looking forward to meeting Cillian. The next, that creep was coming after me.

About half an hour later, the car stops in front of a tall iron gate, somewhat resembling Orla's house gate.

There are no properties around, and from inside the vehicle, I can see a mansion in the distance.

There's a guardhouse at the gate, and even though we're coming on Cillian's orders, the security guard at the gate questions the driver and only after speaking on the phone with someone, probably from inside the house, are we allowed to enter.

I'm not used to having my door opened for me, but this time, I don't even make a move to get out because, as soon as the car stops in front of the mansion, I'm frozen when I see Cillian coming down the stairs.

His face is unrecognizable. Different from everything he's shown me since we first met. The coldness emanating from him is terrifying.

And there's something more too.

Anger.

For the first time, I find myself thinking that that handsome, masculine face is also the last thing many of his enemies saw before they died.

He opens my door.

"Get in, Juno. I'll talk to you soon."

I go into the house, and I think I already know why he's angry. I'm not a security expert, but I understand that my bodyguards failed today. They should have been more alert. It was only me running that might have kept me from getting hurt.

I don't believe those guys would have done anything in broad daylight, but the thought of being subjected to anything, on any level, churns my stomach.

Before reaching the doorknob, I look over my shoulder. Cillian has Hingar pinned against the car, both hands gripping his collar.

I know that the men watching over me aren't from a security company, but members of the *Syndicate*. I also know how they are punished in case of failures. I grew up hearing the stories my cousins told, so what I'm witnessing now doesn't shock me at all.

I enter the house, and for a moment, I forget why I'm here. Curiosity overtakes the unease from what almost happened, and I start making my way to the *hall*.

There aren't many furnishings or decorations. Although the mansion has a more classic style on the outside, the interior is contrasting, what one would expect from a modern apartment. Gray furniture and a lot of metal.

Everything seems hard and resilient. It suits him.

I come to the conclusion that I like the place, especially the huge "v"-shaped sofa in the living room—one of the rooms, I think, because judging by the size of the house from the outside, there must be many others.

I hear the door slam and then footsteps. They stop behind me, and even before I turn around, I can feel his tension.

The last time we saw each other, I was at a disadvantage after all those confessions. Remembering the past always weakens me. Today, even with the fear of what almost happened running through my veins, I promise myself that I won't act like a fragile little girl who needs him to protect her.

I turn to face him, but when our eyes meet, my breath disappears, as if someone had pressed a button, cutting it off.

The effect this man has on me is something I'll never understand.

For God's sake, he's mere steps away and hasn't even touched me!

I was expecting him to talk about the guy who chased me. Maybe about the failure with my security, but never what he does next.

He needs only four steps to reach me.

My heart beats so hard that I swear I can feel the pounding against the thin blouse I'm wearing, and when his hand grips the back of my neck, pulling me toward the mouth I want to kiss, I melt.

A sigh escapes me only seconds before he grabs the lower part of my back, pulling me against his solid body. I tremble with anticipation, and when our lips finally meet, I cling to him as if my life depended on it.

Our kiss is pure lust, but also possessiveness. I feel claimed by him in a primal way, but I want to claim him too.

His tongue explores me, leaving no room for retreat, challenging me to deny his dominance.

I *can't* or *won't*. At this moment, I *understand* that I am his.

He breaks the kiss and looks at me. His eyes seem agitated, no longer the coldness from earlier, but like how I feel: amidst a storm of sensations.

I can't stop, even knowing I'm playing with fire, so I press my body against his as much as I can.

A rough sound comes from deep in his throat, and his thumb runs over my lower lip.

"I like to see that mouth marked by the kisses I give you. I like seeing you like this, swollen and red. Wet from my tongue."

Sweet Lord Jesus!

"I like everything you do to me," I confess, "but I'm also afraid of what I feel."

"Because I am who I am?"

"Not because you're the boss of the *Syndicate*, but because I don't have the experience to handle what's happening between us. But I can't fight what you make me feel. I want more."

"I'm not the right man for you."

I try to pull away, hurt, but he doesn't let me.

"Let me go."

"You don't really want to go far. That's our biggest problem. You don't want to stop me, and I can't stop touching you. Your scent is ingrained in me. Your moans when I kiss you are a fucking addiction."

He pulls me by the ass, making me feel how much he desires me. I wrap my hands in his hair and grip tightly, biting his chin.

"You drive me crazy when you surrender like this, Juno. You know who I am. You should be afraid, yet you surrender."

"Since we met, I've never had a choice. I'm yours."

Chapter 30

Cillian

She has no idea what she's saying, or at least, I don't think she does. My need is no longer just for her body but to possess her completely.

Having her trembling in my arms, receptive and passionate, surrendering total control, has shattered the barriers I still placed on my desire. Hearing her confess, putting herself in my hands, brings me to the breaking point. To a place without laws or rules other than the primal need to take her, mark her as my woman.

"If I make you mine, there will be no turning back," I warn, holding her face.

The days we spent apart weren't by chance. I knew I needed to decide about her, and I couldn't do that if I was seeing her. So, I imposed distance on myself, not even going to see Orla, because I knew Juno would be there.

I'm not a man to hesitate about what I want, but she isn't a one-night case.

"Why would I need a way back?" she asks, recklessly.

The girl has the power to unleash my primitive side.

Bold and feminine, her sensual curves molding, her body surrendering. She is my particular temptation.

I turn her around, one hand holding her neck, the other touching her sex over her jeans.

She moans, and I rub my hard erection against her raised ass, while I bite her neck.

"I will demand everything."

"I'm not afraid. You'd never hurt me."

How much of that is true? How can I promise not to hurt her when my world is surrounded by destruction?

The front door opens, and I hear Kellan calling me, but I still resist letting her go. Juno, however, is frightened and struggles to get free.

When I allow it, she turns to face me, panting.

"Those sons of bitches will be replaced," my brother growls before even seeing us. "They'll spend a month in Central America, watching the fucking grass grow to learn to do what they're told."

Only then, with a third person present, does the fever of my desire begin to subside, and I remember why she is here.

Damn! There must be some kind of spell on the woman. Juno made me completely forget that this isn't a courtesy visit. She was attacked.

"Did I arrive at a bad time?" my brother asks, ironically, behind me.

"No... um... I mean, it's fine," she replies quickly.

Seeing her nervousness and also the embarrassed innocence finally brings me back to reality.

I turn to face my brother.

"I don't want any of the men who were supposed to be guarding her today taking care of the family. Send them to hell, Kellan, but keep them away from me, or I might go back and not be so merciful next time."

"Merciful? You broke Hingar's nose."

"His only fucking job was to watch her, and he failed. He got far less than he deserved."

"I don't think he realized I was in danger." She tries to defend Hingar.

I believe that after weeks of being around him, she somehow became attached to the idiot.

"What happened, Juno?" Kellan asks the question I should have asked, instead of attacking her like a fucking savage.

I want to hear her version, even though I already know who the fucking assholes were that touched her.

"Can I sit?" she asks.

I take her hand and guide her to a sofa. I barely settle her in when Odhran arrives.

"Hey, girl. You don't mess around, huh? Salvadoran mafia. Just got to Boston and already has fans."

"I didn't do anything to make...," she begins.

"Don't worry about answering. He's just being an idiot," I say. "Now, tell me what happened."

"You already know, or you wouldn't have hit Hingar."

"I don't know your version."

She sighs and leans back on the sofa. Before speaking, she covers her face with her hands.

"I was heading to the car to be taken to the bakery for our... uh... meeting. I noticed this group of guys talking a few meters away from me. I was super-protected within my family, but my aunt taught me well whom to stay away from. I pretended not to see them and kept walking. They were saying obscene things. You can get an idea without me needing to explain, right?"

I nod.

"And then what?" I ask.

"One of them reached me. If I had to guess, I'd say he's the leader of the group because he acted with a lot of arrogance. I don't remember exactly what he said. I was really nervous, but I think he asked if I hadn't heard him calling me. I was startled because he was very close to me. I was terrified and tried to run away. He grabbed my arm, and I hit his face with my stuff. I ran, and Hingar came toward me, but not before the man grabbed me again."

She runs her hand over her shoulder and makes a pained expression as if recalling what happened.

"Hingar told him to back off, and when I looked back, he had a knife in his hand."

"Amateur bastard," Kellan says.

"Who was it?" I ask, addressing my younger brother, since I'm sure he's already figured it out.

I only know they are Salvadoran mafia members because Hingar recognized the tattoos on their faces, but that's very vague.

"Joe Pineda," he says.

"And should I know which fucking group this name belongs to?"

"I don't think so. The bastard came to the United States a few years ago, as far as we know, but he's made a lot of trouble since then. He's Fuentes' nephew, the leader of that bunch of idiots."

The Salvadoran mafia has been a pain in the ass for all organizations, even worse than the Mexican cartels, because with them, there's at least some level of control. The *M de Muerte*, their arm here in the United States, takes part in such random and careless actions like the Albanian mafia used to do in the past.

"What do you want to do?" Kellan asks, and I look at him without needing to speak. He knows what's going to happen, but we're not going to discuss it in front of Juno.

"Find him," I say simply.

"Can I deliver the *message* myself?" Odhran asks.

"Yes. Nothing too elaborate. I just don't want him to have the chance to come after Juno."

I look at her, who is paying close attention to the conversation.

"We had an appointment," I say. "Are you ready?"

She seems to hesitate.

"What happened... uh... won't delay the bakery's opening?"

"No. I'll take care of it. I won't let anyone stop you from getting your store. Now, let's go."

I pretend not to notice that my brothers are watching us as I offer my hand to help her up.

When she accepts, I lift her up.

"You have nothing to fear."

"Won't they come after us? Didn't they recognize Hingar or the other guys?"

"Maybe, but it doesn't matter."

She looks at me with a question I can't answer. Juno doesn't need to carry more guilt for deaths. I, on my part, don't value life that much. I can do this for both of us.

Chapter 31

Cillian

"What will happen if those men come after me? Odhran said they're from the Salvadoran mafia."

"Don't worry about that. I'll take care of your bakery's security the same way I do with Aunt Orla's restaurant. She's been running it for over fifteen years, and there's never been an incident."

"How do you manage to prevent them from doing anything against her?"

I turn on the bench to face her.

"You know I can't answer that, Juno."

She averts her eyes, seeming awkward, but her embarrassment doesn't move me. Questions like these in my world mean trouble. The less she knows, the more protected she'll be.

What should I say? That, like with other mafia organizations in the country, I have a considerable number of police and other authorities on the payroll? Explain that they look the other way and pretend not to know that Orla is my aunt and that they also protect her, ensuring their own pockets are always full?

"Enough about those bastards, I want to hear about your store." I change the subject.

"I thought you just wanted to see it."

"No. I want to hear it from you as well. Is everything coming together the way you want?"

She tries to stay serious, looking ahead, probably still upset that I didn't answer her previous question, but she finally gives in and looks back at me, a half-smile appearing on her tempting lips.

"Yes, everything is perfect. Thank you so much."

I hold her hand and feel her shiver. I trace my thumb over her pulse and, when I confirm it's racing with a simple touch, my body responds.

"I can't change the shit from your past, Juno, but I'll make sure that from now on, you have the happiest life I can give you."

She opens her mouth, but at that moment, the driver parks in front of the bakery under construction.

There are a few workers inside, but my men go ahead and send everyone out. Only when no one is left do we enter.

As we pass through the door, Juno can't hide her happiness or proud smile, and it does me a hell of a lot of good.

There's a lot of dust, and most of the furniture is covered with plastic.

I look around and like that she chose everything in light colors.

"Wait outside," I tell my men. "No one is to enter."

She was heading to the back of the property, towards the counter already set up, but looks back when I speak. I see on her face, and from her heavy breathing, that she remembers what happened at my house earlier today.

I lock the shop door and go to find her.

I like watching the way she reacts to me. It's a mix of fear and arousal.

I look at the front of her shirt, and her nipples are pushing through the fabric. Hard and tempting.

"I still don't have a name for the bakery," she says, seeming to struggle to breathe. "I can't decide on one."

I lift her up and sit her on the counter. I position myself between her thighs and move her hair out of the way because that neck is begging for my tongue and teeth.

"Too many options?" I ask, but already completely distracted by her delicious scent.

I nibble lightly on her exposed skin, and she moans loudly.

"How can you expect an answer while doing this to me?"

I pull her closer to the edge of the counter to feel her. I'm as hard as steel and grip her ass, rubbing my cock against the juncture of her legs.

With my fingers tangled in her hair, I kiss her.

Initially, it's a gentle touch, my tongue taking possession of the warm interior of her mouth in an explicit invitation for sex. Telling her without words that this is how I'm going to eat her pussy.

Her breathing becomes short, and she wraps her legs around my back, as if trying to keep me from pulling away.

"Every time you touch me, I feel overwhelmed, possessed. I love the way you control my body."

"Even knowing who I am? Even being sure I have no soul?"

It's not really a question but a final warning.

Wherever we go from here, Juno won't walk blindfolded. She needs to know who she's getting involved with.

I don't expect her to answer. I don't want to give her a choice because my need for her only grows, so I kiss her with urgency and hunger.

My hands close like claws on her thighs, positioning her at the edge of the counter, almost straddling me.

I lift her shirt slowly, giving her time to stop me. I know this is all new to her, and I don't want her to be scared.

The windows, like the door, are covered with paper, protecting us from anyone outside.

Juno doesn't stop me and raises her arms, and when she's only in her bra, I lower my mouth, licking the valley between her breasts.

My fingers slide over the silky skin of her ribs, and she shivers.

I scrape my teeth along her neck, and with one hand gripping her ass, I make her feel my erection.

She pulls me by the neck and I almost lay on top of her. Eager, she grinds against me. Her hips pushing, needy, wanting the relief that only my cock, fingers, and tongue can give her.

"I'm not going to fuck you here. I want you completely naked when I bury myself in this virgin pussy for the first time, but I need a taste of you."

I open her bra and am hypnotized by her large breasts with pink nipples. I lower myself and take one into my mouth while pinching the other between my thumb and forefinger.

She moans and pleads, but I don't think she even knows what she's asking for.

I'm trying to be gentler than usual, but Juno is wild and demanding, grabbing my hair, pulling hard. She's not satisfied with anything less than complete surrender either.

I trace my thumb over her jeans, pressing at her clit, but it's not enough, so I lower myself and bite her pussy over her pants.

The smell of her arousal drives me crazy.

"You're so wet, aren't you? If I pull down your jeans, I know honey will flow into my mouth, Juno. You'll be ready for me."

She sighs and when my fingers return to working her breasts, she goes wild, lifting her hips, offering herself, almost begging me to taste her.

We're in broad daylight, inside a store under construction, but fuck me if I'm not going to give her what she wants.

I unzip her jeans and pull down both her pants and panties. She's at my mercy now, lying on her back on the counter, legs raised, pants around her knees, limiting her movements.

"Cillian..."

"I'm going to make you come. I promised the first time would be with my tongue, and I keep my promises."

I grip her thighs, pulling them even closer. It drives me insane to see her like this, excited, trembling, and exposed.

I bite the back of her legs and run my tongue down, making a trail toward her pussy, delaying, like a kind of mutual torture, the pleasure that's to come.

"Please..."

I slide my hand from her clit to the opening of her untouched sex, and my palm gets sticky with her arousal.

She can't see what I'm doing, only feel, and I think that drives us both even crazier.

I push my thick finger between the soaked folds, not inserting too much, just preparing her.

She moans softly when I lightly bite her sensitized clit.

Her hips gyrate in response, and I hold them tightly, submitting her.

"Say you want me to eat your pussy, Juno. If you're a good girl, I'll make you come in my mouth."

She doesn't say anything, probably out of shyness, and I stop.

My hands move up and down her legs, but avoid touching her sex.

She moans loudly, and I need to use all my self-control to keep from sucking her because she's so wet for me.

The surrender I desire doesn't take long.

"I want everything with you. Only with you. Always with you."

Chapter 32

Cillian

Her words act on me like the most powerful drug. If Juno weren't a virgin, I'd fuck her now, hard and deep, because the desire to be inside her is almost unbearable.

I look at the paradise hidden between her thighs. Her pussy is covered in lighter strands than her hair and is so slick that her excitement shines, waiting for my mouth.

When I lower myself and lick her, her hands grip the counter.

"The moment I take you, I'm going to devour you, Juno. I'm afraid of myself when I start, because I won't stop anytime soon."

I kiss her sex with my mouth open, working my tongue into her tight heat, giving her a taste, like a rehearsal, of what it's like to be fucked.

"This pussy just became my favorite food."

"Please, I don't think I can take much more," she moans.

"It's just the beginning, baby."

I suck on her clit and as soon as I start to slip a finger into her narrow passage, she comes.

Starved, I drink it all in, her pleasure dripping onto my lips and tongue.

I don't want to stop, and I want to hear her scream while my cock fucks her sweet pussy, but Juno deserves more than that for a first time, so when the tremors subside, I dress her again and sit her on the counter.

She pulls me between her legs and arms, covering my face with kisses before reaching my mouth.

It's not something I'm used to. I mean, allowing affection from a woman after sex.

"I wasn't kidding when I said I'm yours. I'm not asking for promises, but while we're together, let's be just us. If what we have ends, let me know, but don't betray me. I couldn't bear going through what my father did, being deceived like he was."

I push her hair away from her face because she didn't look at me when she said that, and I won't allow her to hide, not even in her mind.

I think carefully about what she said. No woman has ever demanded exclusivity from me because they knew that's not how I operate. Juno asking for this only shows how different she is from anything I've ever experienced. Innocent and dreamy.

In her mind, there's no doubt that we're together now, once she gave herself to me. She gave me not only access to her body but her trust.

I should pull away, not because I can't fulfill what she's asking. I know there's no chance I'll want anyone else because, for now, at least, she's the absolute owner of my desire, just as I dominate hers.

What should make me pull back is that getting involved with Juno means leading her through my ugly world.

However, it's no longer a choice. I'm not letting her go.

"I'm bringing you permanently closer to me. I don't know if you have a clear idea of what you're getting into, but I've given you enough time to run. Now, you're mine."

Seattle

One Week Later

TRAVELING WASN'T IN my plans.

I don't handle unresolved issues well, and right now, there are two significant ones directly connected to Juno: finding out who the man was that was in her house the day her parents died and dealing with that asshole who tried to attack her at college.

The bastard has gone into hiding, like the rat he is, which leaves no doubt that he knows he messed with the wrong girl. He or some other member of that gang probably realized that Hingar was Irish, or by now, has already looked into her. It doesn't take a genius to put two and two together.

Evil recognizes itself. It's like looking in a mirror.

I left Odhran directly responsible for her because I can't delegate what I came here to do to another of my men. Not even someone I trust.

The deal with Yerik was closed regarding the six routes for arms smuggling that I demanded from the ex-Pakhan, and that meant I needed to put the entire Syndicate on alert. The moment we take down the first Los Morales man, we'll be officially at war.

Yes, because Ruslan's talk about just getting rid of the Mexicans when they're in our way is not how I operate. Enemies, once declared, don't get the chance to understand what's happening. We're not going to sit around waiting to be caught off guard.

So, I'm sitting with my trusted men, excluding Odhran, who is in Boston, deciding the best strategy to wipe them out.

"These routes we got from the Russians will be crucial for expansion. Since we're just starting arms supply now, we need to show the big buyers that we meet delivery deadlines and can get any type of merchandise they need," Oisin, my secretary, says.

My phone rings and I get up when I see it's Juno.

I gesture for them to wait for me to return and step out of the room.

The same day we went to the bakery, I had to travel, postponing my plans to spend the whole night with her. It's like now that I've decided, life is playing tricks on me, creating obstacles, testing my obsession.

"Cillian?" she asks when I answer.

"Is everything okay?"

She doesn't usually call. She doesn't even text because she knows we can't stay on the phone like regular people would. Even though I change phones every two weeks and we don't discuss anything important in those calls, I don't trust that someone isn't listening to what we talk about.

"I don't want to sound paranoid, but I had a feeling I was being followed at college."

"What?"

"As we agreed, the security guys have been escorting me for the first few days up to the building entrance, but since yesterday, Odhran has been coming with me." She pauses, sounding anxious. "Look, it could just be my mind playing tricks on me."

"Tell me. I'm listening."

I believe that all humans, as animals that we are, have an instinct about danger. I take that seriously and have avoided ambushes by trusting my intuition.

"This afternoon, while walking through one of the empty corridors, I had the feeling that someone was watching me. It doesn't make sense, of course, because those men... they would stand out, and I imagine they don't want to draw attention. Anyway, I'm just saying because we agreed that I wouldn't hide anything from you."

"Good that you called. I want you to do most of your classes from home until I can look into this."

"Okay, but I arranged to meet Elaine at the store tomorrow."

This time, when she mentions the woman's name, I know who she's talking about: the same woman who was attacked by that bastard the only time Juno worked in a fight.

"Don't go to the store alone."

Of course, I'll alert Odhran to keep an eye on her, but she also needs to learn to be cautious, in case the security fails.

"No, it's fine. I won't go without talking to the guys. Do you know when you'll be back?"

"As soon as possible."

"I'm not rushing you."

I don't make a big deal of her irritation at saying that. I know she doesn't like to show any kind of dependency, so I let it pass.

"When I let you know I'm coming back, you'll wait up for me. Rest, baby. I won't let you sleep for days."

After I hang up, I call my brother.

"I was expecting you to call," he says when he answers. "But I can't tell you what I discovered, just know that I'll keep her safe."

"Don't leave her alone."

"Not even when she goes home? It's too tempting."

"Fuck off, bastard."

He laughs.

"Never thought I'd live to see you feel jealous. Don't worry, your woman will be well taken care of."

Chapter 33

Juno

The Next Day

"Do you thank God every night before you go to sleep?" Elaine asks as she walks through my bakery.

Odhran cleared out the workers and the security guards so that the two of us could have some privacy, and now, while I show my only colleague on American soil my dream come true, Cillian's brother waits with the other guys outside.

"He and I don't have a very good relationship."

"How not? Girl, you are the luckiest person in the world!"

I remain silent because she doesn't know anything about my life, other than what I've chosen to share. Otherwise, I doubt she would use the word "lucky" to describe me.

"I talked too much, didn't I?" she asks, but doesn't seem embarrassed. Today is the fourth time we've met, and I'm starting to get used to her direct manner.

"Don't take it the wrong way, but I'm not the type to open up, especially when I've only known someone for a short time."

She reaches out to take my hand.

"I'm not either. I might give the wrong impression because I talk more than bad news, as my grandmother would say, but the truth is that no one knows me beyond the preface."

I shrug.

"What I've seen so far, I like. I don't think friendships need to be rushed. I don't believe in instant love. I'm suspicious of people who love me without any reason. Liking, yes, but swearing eternal friendship after a short time? Doesn't convince me. That's what makes me stay away from social networks. People become best friends or virtual enemies in the blink of an eye when, in fact, no one really knows who the other person is. It's easy to judge someone's life as perfect when we only know them through a profile, but the truth is everyone has problems and fears, no matter how beautiful, chic, or rich they are."

"You're very mature for your age."

"My aunt says I'm a thinker. I don't know. I like to read and it opens our minds. It allows us to see beyond appearances."

"And what do you see in me?"

"You're not as happy as you seem."

"Jesus, and I thought I was the direct one," she says, laughing. "But why do you think that?"

"Because I'm the same way: I let people see only what I want. There are few people with whom I let my guard down."

"At least you have some people to lower your guard with from time to time. That's a safety net. As for me, if I fall, there's no one waiting to catch me."

"I can't promise I'll be the one to catch you. I've never had a friend, but I hope what's starting between us is the beginning of a friendship."

"Me too," she says, looking away. "But I didn't come here to talk about my problems or cry over our sorrows, Juno. Show me your store."

The place isn't very large, but I love it. I was the one who chose it when Orla gave me several options, including some larger spaces, but this one is everything I dreamed of for my bakery.

I mainly show her the kitchen, at the back, equipped with the latest in restaurant technology.

"Alright, you might not have a good relationship with God, but He and I are quite close, so I'll thank Him on your behalf."

"I didn't say I don't talk to God, just that I don't ask for anything anymore."

"Wow, I on the other hand, bombard Him with requests every day." She looks at her watch. "I have to go. I work in the fights today."

"You said you do small jobs during the day, right?"

"Yeah, anything as long as it's not killing, stealing, or prostituting myself, I'm in."

"Like what?"

"Walking dogs, cleaning houses, senior companion services... When I say anything, I mean anything."

"Nothing steady?"

"The most stable thing I have are the fights, and they're what support me. Sometimes they happen during the day and if I had a nine-to-five job, I wouldn't be able to leave in the middle of the shift when I needed to."

"Have you ever worked in a restaurant?"

"Yes, I have. When I was in my first year of college, before I had to drop out."

"Why did you have to stop?"

As soon as I ask the question, I regret it. It's so hypocritical not to share my secrets and then ask a lot of questions.

"Sorry, it's none of my business."

"Because of my son."

I step back to look at her.

"I'm sorry to ask this, but how old are you?"

"Twenty-three."

"I'm not trying to be intrusive, I swear, but you don't look like you have a child."

"But I do."

Elaine rummages through her bag and pulls out her phone. She searches through the pictures and then shows me a photo of a little boy who is the cutest thing in the world, but he doesn't look like her.

"He's perfect, Elaine."

"Isn't he?"

She doesn't talk about the father, and I don't ask. It's obvious they're not together; otherwise, she wouldn't need money so badly.

The boy is a baby, maybe about two years old, if I had to guess. He has dark curly hair and looks like an angel.

"Is that why you have so many jobs?"

"Yes. There's nothing I wouldn't do for my Jax."

I look at her, debating whether I should say what I'm thinking. I quickly decide that my instincts have never let me down, so I'll take the risk.

"Do you want to come work with me?"

Her shocked expression shows she wasn't expecting that.

"What?"

"I need to hire two people, and you said you have restaurant experience..."

"Are you serious?"

"I am. You won't have to give up the fights. When they happen, just let me know in advance."

"Why are you doing this? You barely know me!"

The question isn't aggressive. All I see on her face is confusion.

"True, but I've liked what I've seen of you so far. Besides, I'm not asking you to marry me. It's not a lifelong bond; I'm just inviting you to work here. If it doesn't work out, you can go back to your previous jobs."

"I get that part, but why me? The O'Callaghans could find more experienced and qualified people."

"Orla has already hired someone quite experienced to handle the front counter, literally. Actually, I prefer to stay in the kitchen making my sweets."

"You didn't answer my question, Juno. Why me?"

"You'll have a fixed salary and also health insurance for you and Jax. You said I'm lucky, and I'd never seen my life that way, but maybe, in the end, I am. It's time to give back by helping others."

With all her playful demeanor, I expected some funny quip, but instead, she hugs me, and when I return the hug, I notice she's trembling.

"I'll never forget this, Juno."

I feel very awkward.

"Hey, it's no big deal."

"It is. The health insurance is what worries me most about Jax," she says, wiping her eyes.

"Why?"

"He was born with a heart problem. He can't have surgery yet, but the doctors say it might be necessary at any time."

"Oh my God. Then I'm even happier that you're coming to work with me. Just one thing: the O'Callaghans are going to turn your life upside down before I hire you."

"Nothing they haven't already done when I started working in the fights," she says, drying her tears and smiling. "I told you I've been working in them for a few years, remember? When you start, they check everything and then do a re-check every six months."

I look at her, confused, and I think she guesses what I'm thinking.

"They don't check us for legal problems but for connections with other organizations," she explains.

"Ah..."

Wow, I hadn't thought of that. I still have a lot to learn.

"So, the opening is in three weeks, right? Should I start the next day?"

"Actually, I'll need you here as soon as the construction is finished. The person Orla hired to train me and the other employee wants us to do some practice runs before we open for real, so get ready to eat a lot of *cupcakes* and serve tables for the *Union* guys too."

"Like... As if they were customers?"

"Yep."

"When does the construction finish?"

"Next Monday."

"I'll need to let the people I work for know, especially those I walk dogs for, but I should be free by next Wednesday at the latest."

"Okay. If you're giving me your word, I won't look for someone else to hire."

"I am. I won't miss this opportunity for anything. I just hadn't looked for a formal job before because of the fights, but if you're saying I can continue working in them, then for the rest of the time, I'm yours, *baby.*"

Chapter 34

Juno

Two Days Later

Odhran: "Your babysitter has arrived, my queen. See if you don't take too long to move that beautiful ass out of the classroom because I've got a hot redhead waiting for me."

In the beginning, I was annoyed by these messages because I was sure he hated having to "look after me" for his brother, but then I realized that his bad mood isn't something personal, specific to me; it's a family trait.

I almost regretted talking to Cillian about the feeling of being followed in the college hallways, but then I remembered that the guy who attacked me, Joe Pineda, is from the Salvadoran mafia, so it's better to be safe than sorry.

I type a reply.

"I need to pee. I won't have time to get home."

I send the message with a smile. Despite his rough manner, Odhran doesn't like talking about feminine matters.

Odhran: "Too much information, miss. I'm waiting for you outside the building."

I enter the empty restroom and head to the third stall. I can't explain why; I never use the first one, and the second one is occupied.

Before doing what I need to, I put my phone in my bag because the other day, it was in my back pocket and almost fell into the toilet when I pulled down my jeans.

I finally sit down to pee; I hear the door next to me open and the person inside start washing their hands.

There's a crack in the door, and I can see the shadow of the person at the sink. It's like a kind of secret camera. I watch a brunette adjust her hair and then apply lipstick.

Before getting up, I dry myself and flush the toilet. I'm pulling up my jeans when the door opens again.

A shiver runs down my neck as I hear the footsteps. They're slow and heavy; they don't sound like a woman's. For some reason, my heart starts racing, but it's when the door of the first stall slams against the wall, as if someone kicked it, that fear overtakes me.

I grab my phone and, while I hear the person speaking Spanish on the phone, I send a message to Odhran.

"I'm in the bathroom on the first floor. There's someone here. Come find me."

It's just enough time to send the message, and just like the first time, the door of the second stall is kicked in.

I know the person who did that will soon reach mine, and there isn't enough space for me to protect myself. The gap between the door and the toilet is minimal.

I move as close to the wall as I can, and just as I reach it, my stall door is flung open with a crash.

The man in front of me — actually, a guy who can't be much older than me — doesn't have the tattooed face like the others who attacked me a few weeks ago, but I'm sure they're from the same gang.

"Joe sends his regards, princess," he says, confirming my suspicions.

My first instinct is to attack him, but when he reveals a knife blade, a kind of larger pocket knife, I lose my breath.

"Come on."

"You won't get me out of here. I'll scream."

"No, you won't. If you open your mouth, I'll slit your throat from ear to ear."

I feel like throwing up, but I need to buy time.

"You wouldn't do that. We're in a college. You'll get arrested."

He laughs.

"You think I'm scared? My life is about following orders, and the order was: bring the blonde bitch in alive or dead."

He takes a step inside, but before he can reach me, Odhran appears behind him. It's quick and silent, because I didn't hear him come in.

In the next instant, Odhran's arm is wrapped around the man's neck in a chokehold.

It all happens in a split second, and I can't move, not even when the knife the man was holding falls to the floor.

"Get out and wait for me in the car, Juno."

"Odhran... you can't... You can't..."

"It's not the time to play the rebel, girl. I know what I'm doing."

I grab my stuff, trembling like a green stick and feeling bile rising in my throat.

I don't look at either of them as I head for the door. Outside, there's not only one of my bodyguards but also an older man with a cleaning cart. I know he's a college employee, and I can't hide my surprise.

Is that man also a member of the *Union*?

I don't have time to think, as the bodyguard commands:

"Let's get out of here, Juno."

I can't even say how I managed to get to the car with how much I'm shaking. To my surprise, the driver doesn't speed off, and less than five minutes later, Odhran joins me in the back seat.

I open my mouth, and he shakes his head from side to side.

"Don't ask. Today you got a taste of what it means to be the woman of one of the *Union* members. It's not a pretty life, but you will always be protected. However, note one more thing: for your own safety, silence is crucial."

"I can't pretend that didn't happen, Odhran. I have four more months to study. And what if they come back?"

I hate that my voice sounds shaky, but I can't help it. I still feel terrified.

"Damn it, Juno," he says, pulling me closer with his arms around my shoulders. "That shouldn't have happened."

I let myself stay close because right now, any comfort is better than none, even if he seems upset and I'm not sure if it's with me.

"I'm not giving up my diploma. Am I supposed to stop studying in my last semester because of that animal?"

"Girl, maybe my brother didn't tell you the truth about who those guys are so you wouldn't be scared, so let me explain."

I pull away to look at him because something in his voice tells me I'm not going to like what I'm about to hear.

"Those sons of bitches are all over the place. They usually operate with prostitution, but the idiot who was following you that day likes to play differently."

"I don't understand. Are you saying he wanted me to be a prostitute? Human trafficking, is that it?"

"No. Human trafficking is what his uncle is involved in." He runs a hand over his face. "Shit, there's no nice way to put this, Juno, but you're already a grown-up, so here it goes: if that Salvadoran soldier had managed to take you from the college, by tonight you'd be begging for death. It's not the first time it happens, honey. They'd keep you for days being used by multiple men and in the end, they'd kill you."

The tremors that had started to subside return.

"What are we going to do?"

"You're not going to do anything. The *Union* will take care of everything."

"How?"

"Juno, you already know you won't get answers, so spare us both the headache and focus on trying to reorganize your college schedule to take as many classes online as possible. When you must go in, you'll be with bodyguards the entire time. That's non-negotiable."

I really want to know what happened to the man who threatened me, but he's not going to answer anyway, so I just close my eyes and let them take me God knows where.

Chapter 35

Cillian

That Same Night

I'm not the type to waver on decisions. My life is a straight line. Making decisions quickly is something I handle often, but when I got off the plane and Kellan was waiting to tell me what had happened, for the first time that I can remember, I hesitated.

I already knew something serious had happened because Odhran sent me a message saying he was bringing Juno to my house to "protect her."

However, now that I know they have the bastard who tried to kidnap her, I'm torn between killing him myself or going to meet her.

Normally, the choice would be easy. I like to punish with my own hands those who come near what is mine, and if there's one certainty on this fucking planet, it's that Juno is mine.

This time, though, the desire to see with my own eyes that she's safe wins hands down.

"Tell me everything, now, in detail," I say as soon as we get into the car.

"Odhran was waiting for her to come out. Juno went to the bathroom. Minutes later, she sent him a message saying she was in danger or something like that. When he arrived, there was a Salvadoran threatening her with a knife. He wanted to take her. You know what would have happened if he had succeeded."

I know. If he had been successful, we wouldn't even find a body. There are several cases like this, especially in Florida and the Carolinas.

They kidnap in broad daylight. They don't care about cameras, footage, or getting caught.

We monitor their activities from a distance. They haven't crossed our path until now, so there was no reason for us to interfere, but we know how they operate because the sister of one of their victims, the only survivor, came to work with us.

The girl told my men that her older sister was kidnapped near a mall, taken to a mansion in South Carolina while more than a dozen men took turns with her. She barely escaped.

When they thought she was no longer useful, they took her near a swamp to execute her and then throw her body to the alligators, which seems to be their usual method.

The girl knew she was going to die, so she jumped into the alligator-infested water before they could shoot her. She survived to tell the tale. She named names and gave testimony. Only two guys were convicted, and for lesser charges, because the authorities said there wasn't enough evidence.

As a natural skeptic, I think it's more likely they were paid off to look the other way, making evidence disappear.

The house where the girl was kept burned down and was never investigated, and since she jumped into the water, any biological trace disappeared.

I remember what Ruslan said the day we met: that if a member of *Los Morales* took one of Yerik's kids, he'd set the country on fire. Now I understand him, because if they had taken Juno, I wouldn't stop until I killed them one by one.

"What do you want me to do?"

"The usual. Interrogate him and then kill him. Make it big. A work worthy of an artist. He should be delivered to the territory of those sons of bitches."

"We can't cross the state with a body," he says, since the largest concentration of Salvadorans is in New York and that's where Fuentes, the leader, is.

"They won't need to. As for the body, leave it here, in front of one of Joe's girlfriends' houses. The bastard has been hiding since he found out Juno is protected by us."

"Then I don't get the New York part."

"I'm talking about Fuentes, their leader. The soldier we're going to kill was obeying orders from his nephew, but he's one of his men. Photograph the body and send it to him. The bastard will understand."

"I want to ask you something."

"I don't have time for that right now, Kellan. I need to see her."

"It's about her."

We're stuck in a fucked-up traffic jam and my irritation is almost uncontrollable.

"Speak up already."

"Are you two together?"

"She's mine."

He nods.

"Like, as a girlfriend?"

What the hell am I supposed to say?

There's no explanation for what Juno is in my life, because I've never lived anything like it. I haven't slept with her, and yet, I feel with every drop of my blood that she is my woman.

"What's the point of this question? On a good day, I'm not a patient person, but today my mind is a whirlwind, Kellan, so just say what you need to say all at once."

"I think we can handle the Salvadorans, but we're about to go to war with the Mexicans too, because of your deal with Yerik."

That hits me like acid: *Yerik* and *deal* in the same sentence.

"Go on."

"Joe Pineda knew she was under our protection and still sent someone into the college to try to take her. It sounds like obsession to me. There were many things that could have gone wrong. She could have screamed, someone could have entered the bathroom... We only managed to get their man out of there in Uncle Prim's cleaning cart," he says, referring to the grandfather of one of our soldiers who works at the college Juno attends. I had him reassigned to work in her building. "What I'm trying to say is that someone who takes such risks has nothing to lose. With or without our warning, they won't stop."

"What are you thinking?"

"Claim her as yours. Not as a girlfriend, but as a woman. Your lady. Joe might not get the message, but Fuentes will. He knows that the moment he touches Juno, he'll be dead."

"I'm going to kill him anyway and also that fucking nephew of his. The first time they approached her at the college, they didn't know who she was. Now, they at least know she's under the protection of the *Sindicato*, even if they don't know she's mine. If they don't understand the concept of family, I'll teach them."

"What you're saying aligns with what I proposed. I agree with you. We'll kill them, but for now, we don't need to start an open war. Show her as yours and let them think everything is fine for now, as long as they don't touch her again. And then, when they least expect it, we'll send them to hell."

Chapter 36

Cillian

"**I**s she staying here?" Kellan asks as the driver parks in front of my house.

"Yes. She'll be safe with me."

"Why are you fighting so hard against claiming Juno? It's obvious to anyone that you want her."

"Aside from the fact that I'm almost twice her age and that the girl hasn't lived much yet, bringing a woman into our world isn't exactly something we do with a smile on our faces. We're billionaires, but also prisoners of our businesses. I'll never be able to give Juno a fairy tale life or guarantee she won't be widowed and left to raise my children alone."

"Nobody can guarantee that. Our parents died young. Life is fragile."

"Exactly. My father would have been our uncle's successor if he hadn't died. Instead, I took over and had no choice about being ready or not. I don't mind living the life I lead. There's no other path for me. The *Sindicato* is part of who I am, but Juno still has options. By presenting her to the world as my wife, I'm marking her."

"She's already marked, Cillian. Juno grew up within the *Sindicato*, and that alone would make her different from a regular girl. Now add all that shit that happened when she was a pre-teen. What her fucking mother did can't be erased from memory. Juno is very young, but don't doubt that she knows exactly what pain and danger are."

He's right. Regardless of her biological age, Juno has matured through suffering.

"I've never seen you like this with a woman," he continues. "I understand your doubts, but don't let her slip away. It's clear she's crazy about you."

I get out of the car and watch him drive away, while I take longer than usual to enter the house.

I climb the stairs in front of the porch, delaying the moment I'll see her, because now that I'm finally alone, I can admit that just the thought of something happening to her drives me insane.

I open the door without knowing what awaits me.

Tears? I doubt it.

Fear? Maybe. She wouldn't be human if she didn't feel it.

Nothing prepares me, however, for arriving in the main room and seeing her lying on my sofa.

She's barefoot with her legs drawn up to her chest. Her arms are wrapped around herself, mimicking the day she told me, at her house, about the hell of the year before her parents died.

Her hair partially covers her face, and sleeping, she finally lets me *see her* completely.

The scene affects me so deeply that I can't move.

In her unconscious state, Juno offers me vulnerability.

I told her, the day I devoured her in her pastry shop, that being with me would be a one-way street, but the opposite is also true. I know myself, and I know that once I taste her, one taste won't be enough.

I'm going to consume her, and I don't think the hunger she awakens in me will ever subside. But is that what I want? To be with the same woman for the rest of my life? To start a family? Was that what my father thought when he met my mother?

These are questions I still don't have answers to, but I know that for now, Juno is my desire.

"You're here," she says, surprising me.

Now I see she's awake and has been watching me too.

I don't say anything as I walk to her and lift her into my arms. I carry her up the stairs to my bedroom and head to the bathroom.

"I missed you," she says as I sit her on the bathroom counter.

I can't handle what's going on inside me right now, so instead of throwing words around, I touch her, care for her.

"Cillian?"

"Let's take a shower."

Usually, I already feel filthy next to her, but today the feeling is even more intense.

"Alright."

She lifts her shirt without looking at me, and I can see how embarrassed she is.

"Are you sure you want this? Because I'm not a sweet or gentle guy, Juno. This version that only you have access to is the softest I can be."

"I don't want you to pretend with me. What you are fascinates me."

"You have no idea who I really am," I say as I unbutton my shirt.

She doesn't hide her interest in my tattoos or the desire as her eyes wander over my chest and abdomen.

She steps down from the counter and removes her bra. Now she's only wearing jeans.

I feel my mouth go dry with the desire to take her breasts between my lips.

I know what it feels like to touch her. Her skin is so silky it doesn't seem real.

"Take everything off," I command.

Her cheeks flush, but I watch, almost breathless, as she sheds the rest of her clothes.

Without asking me anything, she goes to the shower, turns on the water, and steps in without even waiting for it to warm up. I suspect it's an attempt to hide, but I won't let that happen. If she wants everything, she'll understand what my everything means.

I've just removed the rest of my clothes and walk over to where she is, facing away from me, the water running down her hair and ass, turning her, in my eyes, into something almost mythical. A goddess.

I wrap my arms around her waist and breasts and go hard at the feel of her soft, feminine body against mine.

She leans her head back against my chest, surrendered.

I start to wash her with my hands, without using soap.

It's more about mapping her body than anything else. I don't want any part of Juno to remain unknown to my hands or mouth.

"I'm insanely turned on, so let me know if I'm going too fast," I say, nibbling her ear and reminding myself that I'm with a virgin.

She turns in my arms, her hard nipples rubbing against my abdomen.

"I'm not afraid of you."

I lift her chin so she looks at me.

"Maybe you should be."

Her face is red, probably from the shyness of being naked with me, but she doesn't pull away.

"You said you wanted a shower. Let me do that. I'm curious."

"About what?"

She swallows.

"About your body. I've been imagining it every night. I feel hot when I think about you naked."

She's embarrassed, yes, but she's also incredibly sincere, which drives me wild. I'll teach her to say everything she wants and likes.

Juno doesn't wait for a response. She grabs the soap and starts rubbing my chest.

The touch is delicate, even uncertain, but it ignites me in a way that being with the most experienced women never has.

I can barely breathe, wanting more, wanting everything, but I'll let her explore my body first. To get used to it, because when it's my turn, I know it will take a long time before I pull my hands away.

Her fingers slide over my skin and when they reach my abdomen, they brush against my cock, which is hard and thick, pointing upwards.

"Touch me."

"How?"

"I'll teach you what I like, but the main thing is that you know I want you to touch me."

Without waiting for her to act, I take one of her hands and wrap it around my cock, making her slide it up and down, masturbating me. I take her other hand and guide it to my balls.

"I'm your man, Juno. You're going to know my body as well as your own."

She moans, and the sound of her pleasure sends a jolt to my cock.

I release her hands and let her learn and explore.

I'm attentive to every movement she makes and throb between her fingers.

"Harder," I command, and she obeys.

When she looks up at me, her pupils are dilated with desire.

"And what else?"

"Kneel. I want that plump mouth around me."

Chapter 37

Cillian

She does as I ask, and I turn off the water without breaking eye contact.

I slide my thumb across her mouth.

"Suck."

I'm unprepared for the hunger with which Juno sucks my finger. It's as if I'm her sustenance and she's about to make her last meal on Earth.

Damn, she's delicious.

I caress her hair with my free hand, tilting her head back.

"You're going to look at me the entire time. I want your eyes on me while I'm fucking your mouth."

She obeys.

God, those eyes of hers are going to be the death of me.

They invite me to dive into her. To take her however I want.

I need to struggle to control the ferocity of my desire. I want her desperately.

"You're trembling, Juno. Just say the word and I'll stop."

She licks her lips.

"No. Teach me."

A rough sound escapes from the back of my throat. Her submission throws me off balance.

Gripping the base of my cock, I brush the swollen head against her lips. She moans, showing that the madness between us is mutual, and parts her lips to take me in.

Looking at me, she licks the tip, as she did with my finger, and then sucks.

The size and thickness of my shaft against the delicacy of her lips is incredibly erotic. The veins, swollen with arousal, are stretched to the limit.

Juno sucks lightly, tentatively tasting me, but even with her inexperience, she's driving me insane.

I move my hand to pinch a nipple, and in pure reflex of lust, she opens her lips wider, allowing me to enter.

I can feel her purity. It's like breathing fresh air. No woman has ever awakened me like she does, enchanting me like a siren's call.

"Open your mouth wider. Slide your tongue along my cock."

At first, she seems shy.

I push her hand away, holding each side of her face, and slip between her moist lips, taking control of the blowjob. I think this is what I wanted because from then on, she surrenders.

And damn, Juno isn't just beautiful, she's incredibly sexy.

It's as if by giving me control, every erogenous zone in her has been activated.

She moans shamelessly and lets me in, though I'm controlling myself from thrusting as hard as I need to.

"So delicious," I growl as I nearly reach her throat, and she gags.

The sound she makes heightens my arousal.

She eagerly accepts me as I devour her mouth, and it doesn't take long before I'm very close to coming.

I lift her up, and I don't think she even understands what's happening as I take her to the bed.

We're wet, a mess, but I don't care. I need her. To enter her body and make her mine.

I lie on my back and pull her over me, being careful not to align her sex against my cock. She's not ready yet.

I run my hands over her body. Thighs, abdomen, breasts, never taking my eyes off her for a second.

"You're beautiful."

Her face turns pink.

"I feel beautiful with you. And complete."

I bring her to my mouth, kissing her lips to prevent her from saying things like that. Juno is worming her way under my skin, and maybe the time will come when she won't leave.

Her hands hold my face, her nails grazing my jaw and neck. Devouring me with the same need I feel for her.

I fuck her mouth with my tongue, moving it in and out, trying to release some of the madness I'm feeling.

It's such a wild pleasure that it borders on pain, so intense is the urgency.

She moves over my body like a snake, sliding, offering herself, pressing her wet pussy against me.

The scent of her arousal quickly becomes my favorite perfume.

Juno trembles in my hands, precious, sweet, and mine as hell.

I lift her, seating her on my face. She looks at me and turns away, very embarrassed.

"Open up your pussy for me. Feed me."

She parts her lips, still hesitant, but when I scrape my teeth against her clitoris, she grabs the bedpost and pushes herself against my mouth.

I grip her ass while I suck her, her drenched sex dripping onto my face.

"You taste sweet."

I can't get enough; I could spend days sucking her.

Her breathing is ragged, and just by the way her sex contracts on my tongue, I know she's close to coming. When she finally unravels, I can't stop.

Summoning nonexistent self-control, I lift her off me and lay her on the bed.

I get up to grab a condom, and when I return, she's still in the same position I left her, but with her thighs together.

I spread her legs and position myself between them, on my knees.

She looks at me, breathless.

I lie down without shifting my weight and place a hand on each of her cheeks, forcing her to keep eye contact.

I lower myself and fit into her pussy, but before I push, I whisper in her ear:

"Mine."

Her sex grips the head of my cock, gradually taking me in, but when I push further, she whimpers.

I pull out of her and slide my hand between our bodies. When I feel with my fingers how wet she is, soaking me in her arousal, I have to close my eyes for a moment.

"You want me inside your pussy, baby. You might be scared, but your body wants to be taken so badly. It's dripping for me, Juno."

She shudders and raises her hips.

I rub her clitoris, giving her a bit of what she wants.

"Guide me inside you. I won't hurt you more than necessary."

Juno spreads her legs even wider in a silent invitation and, shyly, grips my shaft. When she fits me back into her opening, I growl.

"You're so hot and wet."

I don't stop touching her clitoris, and she starts to relax, her tight walls pulling me inside.

Juno is the picture of perfection with her deliciously open mouth, her needy eyes. An angel begging to be corrupted.

I thrust in a slow but steady rhythm, and when I push against the barrier of her innocence, her nails scratch my back.

It's hell for me not to bury myself deeply in her untouched body. The wildest thoughts cross my mind.

I want to take her until I hear her scream my name. To come, filling her with my cum. To pound so hard inside her that I feel it for days.

But this is supposed to be our beginning. I can't scare her, so instead of giving in to my primal desire, I move my hips only to increase her need, making her beg to be fucked.

"More," she pleads.

I press our mouths together in a deep kiss and unable to hold back any longer, in one swift thrust, I'm fully inside her.

The feeling of ecstasy is only diminished by Juno's whimpers of pain, so instead of fucking her hard, I take her in a slow cadence.

I kiss one of her hands and guide it to her sex.

"Feel me inside you. Understand how much you're mine."

"Cillian..."

"Touch yourself while I fuck you. I'll make it so good."

I moan as, pulling out and thrusting back in, my hairs brush against her fingers.

I spend a long time fucking her slowly, but when her whimpers of pain turn into sighs of pleasure, I quicken the pace.

"Touch that sweet pussy for me."

"Oh, God..."

I look down and it drives me mad to see her small hand stroking her clitoris.

"Spin your middle finger in circles. Imagine it's me touching you."

When she complies, a shiver of pleasure hits her, and she throbs around my cock, her body pushing up.

The warmth of her sex, even through the condom, is paradise, and unable to fight my nature any longer, I lose myself inside her.

I pull almost all the way out and almost come when I see the condom covered with her arousal.

The room smells of pleasure, flesh, and lust.

I fuck her hard now, each thrust affirming my possession.

With the same greed, she digs one of her hands into my ass, pulling me deeper into her.

What started gently—what most would call making love—quickly turns into hungry, sweaty, brutal sex.

Skin slapping, sliding, teeth reaching and biting each other. Cock and pussy locked in a rhythm of pure lust.

Her eyes, barely open, let me see the pleasure she's experiencing. Juno is so much more than I thought. She's sensual and shameless. Fiery, demanding.

Her muscles grip me in a sign of an approaching orgasm, and holding back from coming before her almost makes my brain explode.

I lower myself to bite her neck, trying to control the impending orgasm.

"Who would have thought my girl would be so naughty? Are you loving being fucked, angel? Do you like having that pussy filled by my cock?"

She tightens even more around me, showing that she enjoys dirty talk.

Crazy with lust, I suck a nipple, swirling my tongue over the hard peak.

She tenses beneath me and finally gives in, surrendering to the orgasm.

I feel the pressure before the orgasm building up in me, and when she trembles one last time, I let go.

The jets of my semen can barely be contained in the condom, and I'm sure if I were fucking her without protection, it would leak out of her given the force of my release.

Her sex still tightens around me and I savor it to the end, dazed with pleasure.

My body is numb after our release, but I'm not satisfied.

She opens her eyes and looks at me.

"You said I'm yours and that's true, but you're mine too, Cillian. Maybe we won't stay together physically forever, but just as you are with me, I'll never leave you. I've taken a part of you for myself and I'm not giving it back."

Her words aren't a threat; they're a sort of prophecy.

I kiss her instead of responding because deep down, I know she's right.

Once I've tasted the paradise of her body, how can I be satisfied with what I had before?

I'm honest enough to admit that the warning I gave her about getting involved with me being a one-way street has just turned against me.

Chapter 38

Juno

I'm locked in his embrace.

It's the first thing I notice upon waking.

Instead of being startled by someone restricting my movements, I enjoy the feeling of being protected by this wall of muscle.

"I was wondering if I had gone into a coma."

I startle at the sound of his voice and lift my head to face him.

"Almost," I reply, feeling my cheeks heat up.

"Was I too rough with you?"

His face shows concern, his brow furrowed.

"I don't have any experience to compare, but I can say that I enjoyed everything we did."

"I went pretty easy by my standards, but it won't always be like this."

I shiver, not from fear, but from pleasure, remembering one of the positions we used, where he had me supported on my hands and knees while taking me from behind.

"Jesus, baby, you're transparent."

"About what?" I deflect.

"I was recalling yesterday. Your face showing what you wanted."

"Is it wrong?"

"No, but if I fuck you again, I might end up hurting you, and what I want with you is all about pleasure."

Before I can guess what he's going to do, he turns me on the bed and spreads my thighs wide.

"I want to mark every part of you," he says.

I should feel embarrassed for being so exposed, but at that moment, I can't think because Cillian's hot breath is on my sex, his rugged expression so hungry that it makes me shiver.

He holds my hips and, without any warning, kisses me between my legs.

"Tasty pussy," he growls, I think to himself.

He rubs his finger on my clit while making love to me with his mouth.

I whimper and try to escape because I'm almost passing out from pleasure, but he doesn't allow it, keeping my legs apart.

My body takes over, my brain isn't functioning. I'm pure instinct. A woman being devoured by her man.

He massages my clit with his thumb, and I tense up, unable to contain the orgasm. I think he notices because his tongue intensifies its movements.

And even when I surrender, wet and satisfied, my body floating among the stars, he doesn't stop.

His mouth still places small kisses where my thighs meet my sex, making me shiver.

"Hold me," I ask.

He lifts his head and seems to ponder the meaning of my request.

"Please."

He finally rises and lies beside me, pulling me into his arms.

"Was that the right thing to say?" I ask.

"There's no right or wrong. Only the two of us."

"I NEED YOU TO CHECK your classes, Juno," he says as he leaves the bathroom wearing dress pants but with his back bare. "You'll have to do most of the housework."

We spent a long time in the shower, but I came to the bedroom because he was going to shave.

I'm finishing getting dressed—jeans with no panties because I don't have any other clothes—but with the view of his muscular chest, I stop and find myself coveting him.

"Don't look at me like that."

"I'm not doing anything," I say, trying to hide a smile.

He approaches me like a feline.

"The hunger I feel for you won't decrease anytime soon. If you look at me like I'm a juicy steak every time I come near, we won't be doing anything but fucking."

"Speak for yourself. I have a store to open."

He shakes his head, almost smiling.

"You're so shameless."

"I don't know what you're talking about. Sex is a recent topic for me. I haven't learned any seduction techniques yet," I lick his nipple, "not yet."

He grabs a handful of my hair and tilts my head back.

"I'll ask them to bring your clothes here."

"What?"

"We haven't talked about it yet, but you'll need to stay with me for a while."

"I'm not understanding."

"For your protection, we need to show everyone watching that we're together."

"Like a fake relationship?"

He shrugs, and that irritates me a lot.

"I don't think there's a name for it."

I free myself from his arms.

"How long will I need to stay here?"

I can see from his closed expression that he didn't like the question.

"Is it some sort of sacrifice?"

"I didn't say that, but I have my life too. An apartment and soon, a bakery to take care of."

He runs his hands over his face.

"Why are we fighting?"

"We're not. I like definitions. I said we'll make people believe we're together, which means that regardless of what you call it, it's a fake relationship."

He stares at me in silence, and I feel a bit foolish for exposing myself. What did I expect? Eternal love vows?

Maybe.

Not eternal love, but at least for what we have to have a name.

As if reading my mind, he says:

"I don't do relationships."

"I didn't ask you to be my boyfriend," I reply, very upset now and holding back from leaving the room. I remember our conversation on the day of the fight and when he said to respect him just as he does with me. Leaving someone talking to themselves is definitely disrespectful.

He comes to where I am, and his face is closed off.

I back up until I feel the wall against my back.

Cillian seems cold and distant, very different from the man who made love to me all night.

"But it's what you want."

"I don't know what I want. I'm too young."

His hand comes to my jaw, forcing me to look at him because I wasn't facing him.

"Don't play games with me, Juno. I warned you that I'm not a sweet guy."

"I didn't ask for sweetness." I hate that my voice comes out trembling. "I just asked how long I'll need to stay here."

"I told you I don't do relationships, and that's nothing but the truth, but it doesn't mean you're not my woman."

"Why did I give you my virginity?"

He steps closer, removes his shirt, and to my surprise, turns his back to me. Even with everything we shared throughout the night, I hadn't noticed the tattoo that covers his entire back.

"Can you see what it is?"

I'm still upset, but it's impossible to ignore the beautiful tattoo. Due to his pale skin, it looks like a 3D design.

"A tiger and a dragon intertwined," I say, frowning, confused.

He turns to look at me.

"On the day of your parents' funeral, you held a bracelet with a tiger. Maybe the one Grady gave you. I made a promise to myself that I would keep you protected and marked you on my skin to never break it."

I look at him, not knowing what to say.

I'm touched by how honorable this man is. My dark guardian angel. To many, the one who bears the punishment, but to me, he was salvation.

"I didn't know what would happen with us. I never thought about seducing you before seeing you as an adult, and yet, you were already inside me forever. I don't make promises I can't keep, Juno. Relationships are an empty label in my world, so no, you're not my girlfriend, you're my woman. If I protected you before we were together, rest assured that now, the circle will tighten. You've been warned."

"If you're trying to scare me, it won't work. You think I'm fragile because of what I've been through, but that's not true. I lost everything: my father and the innocence of trust. Now, I have you. I know who you are, and I want you just the same. I'm not going anywhere. As long as you want me, I'll be yours."

He looks at me as if trying to find any trace of deceit.

There isn't any. I'm in love, and I can't fight it.

"And if my wanting lasts forever? Will you live in my prison? Because that's what I have to offer."

"If our wanting is forever," I correct him, "the real prison would be staying away from you."

Chapter 39

Juno

Days Later

Tomorrow is the grand opening of my bakery, and tonight we're doing the third run-through before we open.

"Apparently, it's not just my nephews who have a sweet tooth," Orla says, smiling, as some of the men from the *Syndicate* eat an endless amount of *cupcakes*.

"I was remembering the other day that my father also liked them," I say. "Funny, I only remembered that after I became an adult. I was cooking here, and suddenly I recalled him coming home with bags of milk candies. Could that have unconsciously made me want to become a pastry chef?"

"Who knows? Our minds play tricks on us sometimes."

"I feel guilty," I confess, and she seems about to say something, but I gesture with my hand. "This time, I'm not referring to his suicide, but because, little by little, our memories are fading."

"I was married for so long that I almost don't remember what life was like without my husband, Juno, and even so, I feel like I'm forgetting many phases of our marriage. I think it's natural, dear. We'll never forget completely, but dwelling on memories, living in the past, I don't think it's healthy."

"How did you manage to live without your husband? He was the love of your life, right? Because when we lose our parents, as I lost mine, it's terrible, but somehow, it's natural for children to outlive their parents. You, however, had a life together, dreams, and I'm sure, the desire to grow old with your partner."

"I had no choice but to keep living. My boys were orphans, and even though they were all grown up and Cillian was leading the *Syndicate*, they would always be my little boys. When Eoin died, I was lost. Living in the heart of the mafia, I prayed every night that he wouldn't be targeted in an ambush, shot fatally, or even stabbed. I never imagined that what would steal him from me was his heart."

"A heart attack?"

"Yes. A sudden one. The funny thing is, he seemed to be anticipating it. For a long time, he had been preparing his eldest nephew to take his place, even though he was still healthy and full of life. When it happened, I couldn't cry out all my pain. As the widow of the former boss, I had to support my boys within the *Syndicate*. There was no doubt that Eoin wanted Cillian to take his place."

I can feel her pain in every word, though she tries to make the conversation casual.

"How did it happen?"

"During a dinner. I remember complaining to him that we could never take a vacation. I didn't have the restaurant yet, and without children, I was a full-time wife. The boys were completely independent, each living on their own, so I fell into the routine of a middle-aged housewife, bored."

"Not just any housewife, a mafia queen."

"Yes."

"Sorry to interrupt you. Please finish your story."

"He was eating and suddenly stopped. He stared at me as if he was going to retort what I was saying. My husband had a temperament very similar to your man's: few words, cold with most people, me being the only exception, but when he was upset, it was something frightening. I expected a fight, maybe even hoping for one to break the routine, because making up was always worth it," she says, winking. "And then, without any warning, he collapsed onto his plate. I froze, not immediately understanding what had happened, but it didn't take long for the deepest fear I've ever felt to spread inside me."

I feel my eyes welling up with tears, her story bringing back memories that make me very sad.

"I didn't mean to make you cry," she says, hugging me. "I told my story because you said you didn't remember your father. With a husband, I think it's different. I've already forgotten many things I lived with my Eoin, but not the smell of his skin, the warmth of his embrace, or how he made me feel loved. I've told you this before, but running the risk of repeating myself, I'll say it again: living with a mafia boss is not a fairy tale."

"Is any marriage a fairy tale?"

"Good point, but what I'm trying to tell you is that if you have the option not to fall in love with a mafioso, whether he's a boss or a soldier, I'd be the first to advise you: run. In my case, there was nothing more to be done. From the first time I laid eyes on my husband, I knew there would never be another."

"Is that why you never remarried?"

"Yes. Widows of the *Syndicate* often find happiness again after a few years, but for me, I knew it wouldn't work. You can't settle for the shadow of a love after you've found the real thing. And in my heart, there was only room for my husband."

"When did you know you loved him? When were you sure that this feeling wouldn't pass?"

"Can you imagine yourself with someone else? I mean, not now, that you're obviously in love," she says, and I feel my cheeks warm, "but if something happened to him?"

"I wouldn't be able to kill what I feel for him, so if a tragedy were to take him from me, no, I wouldn't be able to be with anyone else. I'm not easily trusting, especially with men. The idea of another touching me disgusts me."

"What would be able to kill that feeling, then?"

"Huh?"

"You said if a tragedy took him away, you wouldn't be able to be with another man. That opens the door to thinking that perhaps there's something that could make you give up on him."

"Betrayal," I answer without hesitation. "If he cheated on me, like my mother did to my father, I would leave without looking back."

"IS THERE ANY LEFT FOR me?" he says, brushing my hair aside and kissing my neck.

Everyone has already left, with only the bodyguards remaining outside.

Cillian is less paranoid about my security, and I wonder if it's because he has already *taken care* of Joe Pineda.

In any case, I've been taking most of my classes *online*, and I feel embarrassed when I have to attend the university because there's always one of the *Syndicate* men accompanying me. I haven't felt followed or seen any of Joe's gang on campus again, but it might just be a coincidence.

He didn't tell me what happened to the guy who threatened me in the college bathroom, and I didn't ask.

As I take a while to respond, he turns me around and sits me on the counter, positioning himself between my legs.

"I'm demanding. You're not giving me attention, woman."

I roll my eyes.

"Yes, sir, *boss.*"

He gives me a light smack on the side of my thigh.

"Where are my *cupcakes*?"

"Maybe I ate the leftovers..."

His look of disappointment makes me smile.

I pull him closer and whisper in his ear:

"Or maybe I left some hidden for us to play with at home."

A second after I say it, I regret it.

That isn't my home.

I try to get down from the counter, but he doesn't let me.

"What's wrong?"

"I'm starting to talk about your home as *ours.*"

His expression hardens.

"And what's wrong with that?"

"I don't want to get used to it. When can I go back to my apartment?"

"It's not safe yet."

I think he will stay in a bad mood, but he surprises me.

"Now, we were talking about *cupcakes*, lots of frosting, and you naked in the kitchen of *our* house. I'm not the type to forget promises."

Chapter 40

Cillian

"**I**s this the result of the sketch?" I ask, dropping the sheet Lorcan handed me onto the table. "It could be anyone."

Even though they used the most advanced technology, the same used by forensic labs to identify bodies without documents, the image before me is of an average guy, around forty-five or fifty, because the artist aged him by ten years to show how he might look, and with black hair. He doesn't even look Irish.

My cousin sits in the chair across from me.

"She was just a girl, Cillian. She got confused when talking to the artist, maybe even mixing up the features of the beaters with the single abuser. Besides, she was drunk."

"Don't remind me of that shit because it makes me want to interrogate each one of my men until I find the one who dared to touch her."

"How do you know he's still alive?"

"I don't know, but I'll never stop looking. Until my last breath on this Earth, I will hunt him down."

"The whole story is so fucked up. I needed to see her face the day we gathered so we could recall the past and go after the guys."

"I'm not doing this to hurt her, but because it's the only way we have to catch him. There are no other leads."

"Let's work on it, cousin. Now, give me at least one piece of good fucking news. The deal with Yerik is working out, right?"

"For now, yes. But I don't trust him."

"And he doesn't trust us, I'm sure."

He stays silent, and I know he has something to say but hesitates.

"What is it?"

"My grandfather made a personal request."

"Fuck me! Every time Ruslan comes with this talk, it's always shit."

"Not always. The deal about the guns was a good one. *Los Morales* are nothing to us. Eliminating them in exchange for the routes was a very advantageous deal."

"I don't like associating with that bastard Yerik."

"We're not associated. But it's not about him I want to talk about, it's about the favor my grandfather asked. Maxim, one of Yerik's trusted men, got married."

"You know who he is, right?"

"Yes, the quiet one."

"That's the one. He married a Russian mafia princess."

"And what does that have to do with us?"

"The girl lost her whole family in a fire. Stepmother, father, and sister."

"Sad, but that's life."

"They didn't find the youngest daughter's body."

"Probably because it disintegrated with the heat or some shit like that."

"No. The fire wasn't strong enough to make the bodies disappear. Maxim had it investigated, and so did I."

"You? Why the hell are you concerned with the Russians' shit?"

"Anastacia, Maxim's wife, is Ruslan's goddaughter. The missing girl, Taisiya, is her half-sister."

"Jesus, the man is really God's relative. When he's not spreading himself as a son and grandson, he's got a bunch of godchildren."

He laughs.

"I wouldn't be surprised if we discover more hidden descendants. Anyway, my grandfather wants me to investigate. I might need to be away for a while."

"As long as you're careful. It's not you going after this that worries me, Lorcan, but crossing our paths with the Russians again."

"I want to do it. It might be nothing, but I need to be sure. And what if the girl was taken? What if she's alive and in the hands of some psychopath?"

"And where does this become your problem? Why the superhero syndrome all of a sudden?"

"I don't like to think of a girl being kept at the mercy of a sicko for almost three years. Besides, it won't be for free. Ruslan said that if you agree, we can close a new deal. Yerik doesn't want to owe favors."

"No, no more deals with the Russians. Although the girl you're looking for is Yerik's brother-in-law, I'll consider this a solo mission of yours. You can take the men you need, but the operation must remain confidential. Yerik can fuck off with his pride. I'm doing this not for him or even for Ruslan, but solely to fulfill your request."

He nods as the office door opens and Kellan walks in with Odhran.

"Are you going to the grand opening?" my younger brother asks our cousin, referring to Juno's bakery opening.

"Yes. It will be a private event. Only family will be there," I reply. "Juno insisted that I go, and I can't be there at the same time as the public."

"Then I'll go. Your wife has fairy hands for sweets."

I nod in agreement.

Not only is she incredibly beautiful and hot, but she also won me over through my stomach.

"How many men will be monitoring the perimeter?" I ask.

"Two dozen," Kellan replies. "But I don't think we have anything to worry about. After we dumped that bastard's body in front of Joe's girlfriend's house, he disappeared."

"Besides, it looks like Uncle put a bounty on his head. Fuentes doesn't give a damn about family, not even his own. He only cares about profit, and Joe was starting to draw attention."

"I don't trust Fuentes or anyone who traffics people. I want them all dead. It will be the only way to keep Juno completely safe."

I'm checking my phone to see if there's any message from her when I notice the three of them are silent. When I look up, I catch them smiling.

"Care to share the joke?"

"It's not a joke, but it's amusing to confirm what we all noticed from the first time you reunited with her."

"What the hell are you talking about?"

"Juno. You're completely smitten with her."

"Fuck you three. Don't you have anything better to do?"

"We do. Devour your lady's *cupcakes*."

Chapter 41

Cillian

"You seem restless," she says in the middle of the grand opening of Delícia Doce, her bakery.

"I don't like crowds."

"We only invited those on the list, and all the names went through your brothers' screening. What's wrong?"

I intertwine our fingers and lead her to the room that serves as an office.

Once we're inside, I lock the door and go to a small couch, pulling her onto my lap.

"I think I misjudged your size when I bought the furniture."

"I think so. I'm not sure if I can find a position to fuck you here."

It's more of a tease than a plan. We're both insatiable, but I don't intend to fuck her with almost two dozen people outside.

"You won't know if you don't try," she says.

It's like throwing gasoline on a fire. One thing I've learned about us is that we go from zero to sixty very quickly.

In one second, we're on the couch; in the next, I'm bending her over the desk and lifting her dress.

"Say you planned this."

She laughs, and I get my answer. Juno is wearing a black thong that leaves her delicious ass exposed, as if begging to be bitten and spanked.

"I'm not going to incriminate myself. I have a constitutional right to silence..."

I kneel, pull down her thong, and, spreading her full cheeks, thrust my tongue deeply into her pussy.

She moans loudly.

"You can't scream, *baby*. Your guests are out there."

"Then don't provoke me like this."

"In what way? Am I not supposed to lick you like this?"

I suck on her pussy while massaging her clit, and only when she's very close to coming do I stand up.

I open my pants, grab her hips, and thrust fully into her warmth.

We both moan.

I slide my hand between her thighs, spreading her lips, and caress her hard little button.

She writhes, and I cover her mouth while pounding hard into her body.

"I like fucking you naked. I enjoy seeing you while I'm buried in that tight pussy."

She murmurs against my hand, and it turns me on even more to restrict her.

"I can't understand what you're saying, love. Want it deeper?"

I thrust my hips, and she bites me.

Juno is raw and wild. She loves it when I fuck her hard.

"Will you behave if I uncover your mouth?"

She looks back, and I can tell she's smiling.

I use the hand that was muffling her screams to pinch her hard nipples. She moves, meeting me halfway.

"Harder," she asks. "Ahhhhh..."

I thrust deeply, but it's not enough to satisfy my craving, so I lift her up, sit on the desk, and make her ride me.

"Ride me, hot stuff."

I spank her ass, and she reciprocates, kissing me passionately.

"I have a surprise, but I'll only tell you when..."

"When what?"

"You know."

"Do you want to come?"

"Yes, but I want to come inside you."

"Fuck, woman, you know exactly what to say to drive me crazy."

She rides hard, enjoying it. I'm on the brink of coming, so I take her to a wall, turn her around, and fuck her from behind.

"Mine."

"All yours. I'll never want another man touching me."

Her vow drives me to the edge.

"Come with me," I say, massaging her pleasure spot, "I want to feel you squeezing my cock."

"Oh my God..."

"Come for me. Wet my cock, my woman."

The words seem to drive her wild. She pushes hard, and I reciprocate, making our fuck almost violent.

"I want you screaming in our bed tonight, Juno. I want to hear you begging to be fucked."

The sound of our bodies slapping together is so loud that I have no doubt anyone on the other side of the door would hear it.

I don't know how long we lose ourselves in pleasure. Every time I'm inside her, I don't want to pull out, not just because her pussy is delicious, but because it makes me feel complete.

"Give in," I command, biting her ear.

"I'm going to come," she warns, and at that instant, she starts to contract around my cock.

I fuck her hard, with long strokes, savoring every last second, but just as I'm about to pull out, she turns her face to me.

"Fill me up, Cillian. From today on, we can."

That's all it takes for me to lose control and spill everything inside her.

I've been dreaming about this for days. She went to the doctor to start taking birth control.

Even after the orgasm, I don't pull out, staying connected to the delicious sensation of Juno being wet with my sperm.

"It was a surprise." I smile as I pull her face to kiss her.

My heart pounds in my chest at what I'm about to say, but seeing her today doing what she loves, serving her sweets to the guests and smiling, made me realize I'd die if I had to to ensure Juno's happiness. No one will hurt her again.

"I can't lose you."

I don't know if these are the right words, but I've never declared myself to a woman before.

"Cillian?" she asks, looking worried.

"Wait here."

I zip up my pants and head to the bathroom. I wet a towel in the warm water from the tap.

"Turn around, let me clean you."

I clean her thighs and pussy, and after tossing the towel into a basket, I lift her up and lie on the small couch with her on top of me.

"What was that about?"

"You asked why I was thoughtful earlier. What I said was only partially true. I don't like large gatherings, but it wasn't just that."

"What, then?"

"I'm not going to stop you from having your shop. I see how much it makes you happy. You were born to run a kitchen. I've never had a better *cupcake*."

She blushes, and despite the heavy conversation, I smile.

"You're unbelievable, *baby*. I talk dirty to you while I fuck you, and you ask for more, but just a compliment about your sweets and your cheeks are on fire."

"Your opinion means a lot to me."

"Don't you already have enough validation from my family?"

"Yes, I know they love my sweets, but you're the only one I'm in love with. You don't have to say it back, but I had to tell you. I'm in love with you. Now that I've said it, continue what you were saying," she says, as if giving me her love is no big deal.

Chapter 42

Cillian

I'm completely lost in the plot.

Of course, I knew Juno was as involved as I was, but I wasn't aware of these feelings.

It changes everything. It brings a much greater responsibility.

"I want you to achieve your dreams," I say, and I'm sure I'm saying the wrong thing, but my mind raced with her declaration and all I can think about is protecting her even more. "Maybe I can't give you all of them because of my lifestyle, but the ones I can, you'll have."

"I'm not that ambitious. I'm happier than I thought possible. I guess maybe I'm not good at putting feelings into words, but I'm thrilled with the bakery. Earlier today, I talked to my aunt Eimear. She called to congratulate me on the store. I thanked her in my own way, you know? I mean, I don't know how to be very enthusiastic. I was never encouraged to show emotions, except for the brief time I spent with my father."

I brush a few strands of hair that escaped from her ponytail and tuck them behind her ear.

"Not to me. I see you whole, Juno."

"Because I've always been yours," she says, without hesitation. "I don't wear armor against you. Since we met again after I became an adult, I've never been able to hide from you like I do with most people. What I'm trying to say is: thank you so much. I'm happier with the store than I can explain."

"I know, *baby*, and that's why, so you can keep doing what you love, you have to promise me you'll follow the protocols my men set for your safety."

"Did you read the list they made?"

"Yes, I did."

"Some things are a bit ridiculous. Like, they don't want me to take out the trash to the back of the store, that alley behind. It wouldn't even take me fifteen seconds to do that."

"Look at me."

She lifts her head from my chest when she realizes I'm serious.

"This isn't a joke, Juno. You might think a lot of what they advised you is trivial, but it only takes one slip-up for you to get kidnapped. Besides the obvious fact that I have enemies, we still haven't caught Joe Pineda."

"I'm not suicidal. I won't put myself at risk."

"I didn't say you're suicidal. For a normal girl, your behavior would be quite cautious. The bad news is that you're not a normal girl; you're my wife. We made it public to protect you, and I'm sure that leaders of other organizations will never touch you now that they know you're mine, but the same can't be said for that idiot Joe. I want your word that you'll never put yourself at risk."

"I won't. Why would I take risks if I have everything I've ever wanted?"

"Being the first lady of the Irish mafia?"

"No. Being happy. I don't care if you're the boss. You could be a soldier, and I'd want you just the same."

"Is that what you want forever?"

She looks away from my eyes.

"I'm not asking for an eternal commitment; I'm saying that at this moment, I feel happier than I've ever been in my entire life. I'm also the daughter of a mobster, don't forget, and not a *regular girl*, as you put it. I lived this reality even when I was in Ireland."

I run my hands over her back because she's agitated. Maybe as much as I feel.

Earlier today, while Juno was greeting her guests and moving from table to table, I was studying the place.

I had one of my best shooters assess the property from the outside to make sure it was secure. The windows are bulletproof, but that would only help if the threat came from the street, not if someone came in and tried to take her.

No, not even Joe, that son of a bitch, would risk that.

"What are you thinking?"

"No one will do anything to you inside the store. I have more than my men watching you," I say, without explaining that the police will also be keeping an eye on her for me.

"Then there's nothing to worry about. Outside, I have *my boys*. Or your *men*, as you call them."

She smiles, and I know it's because she's trying to calm me down. She can sense my tension.

Just as I've learned to know her, the reverse is also true.

"Nothing will happen to me," she says.

"It won't, because if it does, Boston and New York will go up in flames."

"Why New York?"

"You don't need to know the details."

"You say I'm your wife, but you leave me completely in the dark."

"For your protection."

"We better get back to the party," she says, irritated.

She tries to stand, but I stop her.

"New York is the headquarters of the Salvadoran mafia."

She relaxes again.

"They won't touch me because I won't give them a chance. I'm a survivor, Cillian. I won't die at the hands of some punks."

"You won't die at the hands of just anyone. You'll have a long life, children, and grandchildren."

The picture forms in my mind as I speak, and for the first time, I realize that I want all of that with her.

The family I knew I would have one day, I finally concede, can't be with anyone other than my Juno.

I'm lost in thoughts about the future when she lifts her head from my chest again.

"Where is that ring you wear from?"

"What?"

"That green stone ring you wear on your left hand. You never take it off, even in the shower. Tell me about it."

She sits on top of me, furrowing her brow.

"It's a tradition within the *Union*. All elite members have one. Mine belonged to my father. Why?"

"No reason, I just think I've seen it somewhere before."

"Seen it somewhere before? You see me wearing it every day."

She shrugs.

"It might be my imagination, but I even dreamed about your ring. I don't remember if my father had one."

"He didn't. Grady was just a soldier."

"Then maybe I'm mixing things up. The jewel is beautiful, and maybe I'm confusing it like I did with the composite sketches. My memory isn't as good as I thought."

I don't respond because my mind is already two steps ahead.

"Cillian?"

"Try to remember why that ring won't leave your mind, Juno. There must be a reason."

"Alright. I'll try, but can we go back to the store now? They must be wondering where we are. Besides, I need to rescue Elaine from Odhran's seduction. If your brother makes me lose an employee and friend, I'll kill him."

Chapter 43

Juno

One Month Later

"**P**erfect!" I applaud myself as I finish decorating the last *cupcake* of the order we'll be delivering later.

"You know what I love most about you?" Elaine asks beside me.

"We'll be here until dawn if you start listing things."

She laughs.

"Your modesty," she says, swatting my butt with a dish towel.

"Are you going to tell me it doesn't look gorgeous?"

I can hardly believe the success my sweets are having.

We can't keep up with the sales because customers keep coming in. Besides the regulars, there are also the men from the *Union*. Even their wives have been coming. I thought the kitchen would be enough for production, but we're also getting orders for parties, in addition to supplying Orla's restaurant.

Yesterday, talking to Cillian about it, he said we could start thinking about a separate factory if I want to supply for large parties, and then I could keep the bakery kitchen solely for the public.

"It is. Congratulations, Juno. Your shop is a success. But I didn't expect anything less. Since I tasted the first *cupcake*, I knew there would be a line of customers. How many people can say they have the privilege of making a living doing what they love?"

"My heart is almost in my throat."

"Why?"

I point to the tray of cupcakes.

"This is my first official order for a party, and I want everything to be perfect."

On the second day the shop was open, a customer came in and ordered a *cupcake* and a coffee. The woman was dressed quite formally. Knee-length skirt, blazer, and a bun. She looked just like those TV show promoters who cover daily court proceedings.

She didn't say much, except to compliment the sweets. Usually, customers chat a bit, even if it's not anything deep. They want to know how long we've been open, things like that.

The woman seemed a bit tense when she arrived, but after tasting the sweet, she even smiled.

The next day, I received a call from her. I was startled and took a moment to remember who she was. She introduced herself as Julie Ramson and said her boss, Dr. Samantha Lambertucci, would like to order one hundred and fifty cupcakes for her youngest son's birthday.

I was incredibly nervous. It's one thing to serve one at a time to the public, another to take an order for so many sweets and decorate them perfectly for a party.

I felt a bit more secure when she told me that on the day she was here, she took one of the sweets to her boss and she loved it, but still, my stomach is in knots.

"You fake it well, then. On the outside, you look like the picture of confidence."

"It's not something I do on purpose."

"What?"

"Faking. It's a habit. I'm not used to letting my feelings show."

"Unless the target is the boss, right?" she says, referring to Cillian.

The first time he came in here while Elaine was here, I thought she was going to have a heart attack from how nervous she got. That's when I realized how people fear him.

I mean, I know who he is and how respected he is, but to me, he's always been in the role of protector, and now... lover? I'm not sure what to call it, and maybe it doesn't matter, because in the end, he's mine. The fact is, I've never felt fear from him like I see other people do.

"As for Cillian, there's nothing I can do. I'm in love."

"You *are*, right? I don't even know if that's the right term or if men like him fall in love, but you don't need to be a keen observer to see that you both breathe the same air. The sexual tension between you two is almost indecent."

I feel my face flush.

"That's passion, not love," I say.

"I wouldn't know how to tell you. I'm no expert on the subject, but I'll speak on what I see: the man is crazy about you."

"It's completely mutual."

Elaine knows bits and pieces of my story, but not everything. Even though I'm growing fonder of her, I don't feel confident enough to open up completely.

"Aren't you afraid?" she asks.

"Afraid of what?"

"I don't want to be intrusive, but men with his lifestyle... I don't know, it's like being married to a cop. There's a sword hanging over your head every day. The wife never knows if her partner will come home."

"The alternative would be not being with him, which for me isn't an option anyway. The love I feel for Cillian isn't something I can give up. I know I'll never feel anything like it again. Maybe what he does isn't the ideal profession for a life partner, but I don't believe in perfect people. Actually, I prefer sinners. Saints don't exist, only those who hide their sins well."

"I wasn't trying to be nosy or puritanical. I know how rotten the world can be," she says enigmatically.

Our friendship is strange. Confessions come out slowly without either of us having to push or make the other feel uncomfortable.

"Everyone is who they are, Elaine. I didn't judge my father because I grew up in that world" I told her my father was a soldier in the *Union* "and I don't judge Cillian, even knowing his world isn't the world of the good guys. I see who he is, and I want him just the same."

"Building a life, you mean?"

I sigh, tired of lying to myself.

"Yes, I want him forever. The American dream. House, kids, dog."

"You already have a house," she says, smiling.

Since I started staying with Cillian due to Joe Pineda's threat, he's never let me go back to my apartment. At first, I tried reminding him that I had my own place, but gradually, I stopped pretending it wasn't what I wanted.

"His house, not ours. I won't consider what we have a commitment until he puts it into words."

"I understand. We women need all the dots on the 'i's, right?"

"I speak for myself: I don't like anything left unsaid."

For a long time, I wanted to believe in my mother's love for me, forgiving her for never saying she loved me, but accepting that she did, settling for every crumb, until she gave me irrefutable proof that she never loved me but saw me as an obstacle to the life she wanted to have.

I no longer accept anything halfway. If he wants me in his life as I want him in mine, he'll have to make it clear.

"Are you going to take the *cupcakes* to him today as planned?"

"I am. I want to surprise him. Our sweet playtime is so much fun."

"So much information, boss," she says, laughing.

"And what about you?"

"What about me?"

"Don't hide it. I've seen that *Mad Lion* is becoming my biggest customer, without a doubt. Maybe his interest isn't so much in my *cupcakes* but in the waitress."

She was smiling but becomes serious when she responds:

"I won't deny he's handsome, but besides the fact that I'm not looking for romance, he's not the kind of man I'd want to get involved with. All the girls I work with and have worked with in fights have been with him. If I were only interested in sex, he'd come highly recommended."

"But you're not," I affirm.

"No. And as I told you before, where I earn my bread, I don't eat the meat."

"Has he ever tried?"

"Not before I came to work here. Because of Jax, I've always kept to myself, even while almost naked during the fights. I'd go, do what I had to do, and return to my son. I think Odhran is so used to women throwing themselves at his feet that he doesn't want to make an effort to win one. I never gave him the opening like the others do. He never came after me. End of story."

"End of story? I swear I understand not wanting to get involved in a temporary romance, but I don't think he'll give up so easily."

"I won't give him a choice. He'll have to use that sexy body of his to satisfy other girls. This one here is not interested."

Chapter 44

Cillian

"Well, now that your stint as the Russian superhero is over, you'll be staying home for good, I hope," I say grumpily to my cousin.

"Yes, I fulfilled my promise and brought the girl back to her family."

"I know you."

"I don't know what you're talking about," he deflects.

"You can't even take care of her from a distance, Lorcan. The girl belongs to the Russians. Don't cross the lines."

He throws himself into the armchair and tilts his head against the backrest.

"Rationally, I know that, but I can't help feeling responsible for her."

"You did what you had to do. You went, saved the damsel in distress, and as far as I know, the dragon was killed," I say with irony. "Fairy tale's over."

He doesn't respond, and my suspicion grows.

"Wait. Are you interested in her in any other way besides the superhero syndrome?"

"Of course not. If it weren't for the fact that she's just a girl, after what she's been through, I think the last thing she would want is to get involved with a guy. Also, don't forget that when she was kidnapped, Taisiya wanted to be a nun. For God's sake!"

"People change, especially after going through shit like that."

"No. She already said she wants to stick to the original plan and go to the convent. Why the hell are you obsessed with this?"

"I'm not. As fucked up as everything she's been through is, it's not our problem. My only concern is with you."

"Why?"

"Because I know you almost as well as I know myself. You still feel responsible for her, even now that the girl is safe with her family."

"I can't help it."

"You can do better than that, Lorcan. If the girl is Maxim's sister-in-law, she's under the Russians' protection. Anything between you, even a simple friendship, will be unfeasible. This deal with Yerik will end any moment now. We were never allies, and we never will be."

"I'm not going to start a war, if that's what you're thinking, but I'll always keep an eye on her. Nothing will change that."

"Fuck me, there must be some kind of disease in this family," Kellan says, laughing as he walks into my office. "Since when did we stop being the bad guys and become superheroes? Each of you has fallen for a damsel in distress, but from where I'm standing, deep down, you're the ones who need protection... — he pauses dramatically — from love."

"Talk about your brother. My relationship with Taisiya is fraternal."

"Uh-huh. Well, I didn't come here to play the fucked-up love therapist, but to talk about the ring."

"What ring are you talking about?" Lorcan asks.

"Juno talked to Cillian about the ring we wear."

He looks at his own hand, observing it.

At first, only family members had one. It's exclusive, made by a jeweler who worked for the *Union*.

Then my uncle decided that all elite members should have one, which led to more than a dozen being ordered. However, when I took over, I suspended that order. They will now be passed down from father to son. No more will be produced.

"And what about it?" Lorcan asks.

"The first time she mentioned that memory, she was just curious about the ring, but since then, I've been pressing the issue," I say. "Three days ago, she told me she's sure the bastard who tried to assault her was wearing one."

"The man who touched her is one of the elite? Fuck me!"

"It wouldn't be the first time we deal with pedophiles among us," Kellan adds.

"Are they already investigating?"

"Yes, and I have six names. Of those, there are three possibilities."

"And what are you waiting for?" he asks.

"Whoever did this covered their tracks very well. In theory, none of them had any connection with Grady or Doireann. They are all trusted men. There's no room for maneuver. If I go after the wrong guy, I'll commit an injustice and lose a loyal member, because there's no doubt he'll be killed," I say.

"And also, if we get the culprit wrong, it will serve as a warning to the real bastard," Kellan adds.

"Let him know he's being hunted," Lorcan says after a moment of silence.

"What?"

"Juno might not remember, but I'm sure the person who did this to her knows she's Grady's daughter. If they haven't acted to get rid of her yet, it's because she's under their protection."

"And more than that: she's his wife now," my brother adds.

"Exactly. Make him start jumping. Call them all for a meeting today and tell them that all elite members will have their pasts investigated. He'll end up revealing himself."

THREE HOURS LATER, I face half a dozen of my men while my cousin delivers the speech we rehearsed about being on the hunt for a traitor.

All present are trained, like us, not to show emotions, and there's nothing on their faces that betrays fear.

However, I like Lorcan's plan. He's right. Whoever is guilty will soon expose themselves because they know they've fucked up. It's just a matter of time before I get my revenge.

When it happens, I'll savor every second.

The meeting ends, and after a few minutes, only the four of us remain.

"So?" I ask.

My cousin shrugs.

"The man who did this is used to hiding."

"Yes. The first thing I did was check if any elite members had an interest in children or teenagers. I found nothing."

"Not even online activities?"

"Not on the surface."

"I can dig deeper. I know people who work in the *deep web*. No matter how well he hides, if he's a pedophile, we'll find out."

"And how are you sure it's a pedophile and not just a one-time incident in the bastard's life, like 'circumstances make the thief'?" Odhran asks.

My cousin shakes his head from side to side, indicating no.

"I worked with a criminal profiling expert."

"He wasn't very good at his job, or he would have figured out who you are," Kellan mocks.

"Or maybe he wasn't sure. I'll never know. Anyway, as I was saying, from the time I worked with that guy, I paid close attention to how he formed profiles, especially of sexual criminals. According to him, for a regular man, an interest in teenagers might be somewhat acceptable, but in children, no. Remember Rick? He beat Juno, but when that bitch Doireann ordered him to molest her, he refused because even monsters have limits."

"Just like us."

"Exactly. A man doesn't become a pedophile overnight. I'll never defend that bitch of her mother, but what we need to think about is: what made Doireann ask her lovers to beat her daughter before escalating to sexual abuse?"

I stand up, understanding where he's going.

"Are you saying that the man we're looking for is the one who put the idea in Juno's mother's head that it would be fun to molest her?" I ask.

"You told me she wanted to be your first lady. Since she didn't get that, she might have aimed for a lower target, but still important. To please her lover, she agreed to offer her daughter as a bargaining chip."

"I hope she's burning in hell," I say. "I'll never stop regretting that she's not alive so I could make her pay, but that son of a bitch, when he's in my hands, will beg to meet the bitch. He'll find death a reward."

Chapter 45

The Devil Incarnate

The noose is tightening.

I knew they were getting closer, but I still thought I could stay in the shadows a bit longer. Eventually, Cillian's obsession with that little bitch would end.

He never sticks with just one woman. Why would it change now?

I must be incredibly unlucky for the head of the Syndicate to get involved with the one I need to kill.

The problem is, the bastard doesn't give any openings.

The girl couldn't be a bit rebellious, disobedient? No. The bitch does everything he says, like a little pet.

I've been keeping tabs on her since she returned to the United States. For starters, she shouldn't have gone so far away. If Cillian had listened to Oisin that day at the funeral, it would have made my life much easier.

Here in my country, it would be easy to eliminate her. He wouldn't be so vigilant because he wouldn't know who I am yet. Now, I have no doubt he has found out.

Why hasn't he come after me? Maybe because he's not sure, and I need to make sure he never will be.

When the girl became Joe Pineda's object of desire, I thought I had struck gold, but besides being fucking overprotected, the girl is smart. She was obedient and stayed under her protector's wings. She probably offered herself to be fucked, enchanting my boss.

Boss, yes.

Too young. A boy, actually. Oisin should have taken his place. Much more prepared and, besides that, he wouldn't come after me just because of my preferences. If I do what I'm told, what's the problem with enjoying the younger ones?

Women never interested me. In fact, Oisin has a granddaughter who is a hot piece. However, once, I made the mistake of getting involved with someone from work by fucking Doireann to get to her daughter. I won't make that mistake again.

I remember the first time I saw her.

Not her fucking mother. Fucking Doireann was a damn sacrifice.

I'm talking about the little blonde angel.

It was at a Syndicate barbecue where I shouldn't have even been.

Normally, I wouldn't have looked at her twice, as my activities are not well accepted by society and could jeopardize my position at work. But I became obsessed with the girl's purity. I needed to make her mine.

She had sad, needy eyes, and I quickly understood why.

The men would talk about how they took turns in her mother's bed while Grady, the cuckold, was traveling. Probably, the daughter knew what Doireann was doing.

I approached her and only needed five minutes to win over the mother. I could see in her ambitious eyes how much the bitch was salivating to become the lover of someone powerful. And if I needed to get to her to reach the girl, so be it.

After I started fucking her, I began planting the idea in her weak mind that the girl needed to be disciplined. I knew she had other lovers, so I convinced her to let them beat the daughter.

I don't hit children. I love them. Each one who has been with me was cherished until the end.

The end.

A pity it had to happen. I would love to keep my harem of little slaves, but it was a risk I wasn't willing to take.

But I'm digressing. Losing track of my plans.

I've been like this lately. Always scared, thanks to that damn Cillian.

Going back to Doireann, I gradually instilled in her weak mind the idea that beating the daughter wasn't enough discipline and that she needed to make the girl grow up.

It's true I didn't have to put in much effort. She told me that because of Juno, she hadn't become the Syndicate's first lady. She hated the girl, and I think my plans just aligned with her most twisted desires.

But the cow got ahead, betrayed me, and allowed one of her boyfriends to almost take what was rightfully mine. If Rick hadn't been a coward, he would have been the first.

I beat Doireann for daring to do anything without my orders, and the next day, I went to her house for the first time. Until then, I had only seen her in hotels. I didn't trust myself to be so close to Juno and not take her forever.

Because that was my intention.

I didn't want to touch her occasionally, but to make her my personal toy. Secretly.

I would have to kill Doireann, of course, but who would miss that bitch? Certainly not Grady, the cuckold.

To cut a long story short, I convinced Doireann to get her drunk when I went to her house, but even that the bitch couldn't do right. The girl woke up, ran away, and the rest is history.

The phone rang, and Doireann said we would have to leave it for another day because Grady was coming home.

I almost ran. An indignity for a man like me.

I hid like a rat, and what's more fucked up, the "other day" never came.

Grady killed the bitch and then killed himself.

Still, frustrated at losing my angel, I'm the type who covers his tracks. Even though the girl was drunk, she might eventually remember.

I don't usually leave witnesses, so when she was sent to Ireland, I waited for the right moment to kill her. I never had the chance. They were obsessively watching her.

Life is a fucking strange game.

The pieces mix up on the board. Rules are broken.

Suddenly, everything got out of control when she not only came back here but became the boss's woman.

Now, I need to be quick. I don't have much time. Every minute lost is working against me.

Chapter 46

Juno

"You don't need to come up with me, for God's sake. Haven't you heard of the concept of privacy?" I say to my security as we enter the building where Cillian's offices are located.

I'm carrying a small basket with sweets and also some toys that I plan to use.

It's not the first time I've come to his office after hours, and if past experiences are anything to go by, we're going to have a lot of fun.

"You know we can't let you go up alone, Juno."

"It's supposed to be a surprise. I was going to take the stairs. If we use the main elevator, he'll see us arriving through the cameras."

"No."

I roll my eyes.

"If you want to follow me, then we'll all take the stairs."

They look at me disapprovingly but know I won't back down. I'm not one to cause trouble, but sweet Lord Jesus, this is Cillian's building, literally. I don't think even the Salvadoran suicide would come in here.

"I'll go up with her," Lorcan says, appearing out of nowhere.

I'm surprised, both to see him and to have him offer to keep me company. Of all Cillian's relatives, he's the quietest.

I'm so shocked that I just follow him to the stairs without saying a word.

"Why are you doing this?"

He grabs my arm and stops me.

"I'll explain."

"Start now, because if you don't, I'm not going anywhere with you."

He looks offended.

"Do you think I'd hurt you? Cillian is like a brother to me."

"No offense, but my loyalty and trust are with him and no one else. If you don't tell me why you're coming up with me, I'll start screaming like a madwoman."

"Jesus!" He gives his first *almost*-smile since we were introduced, and the pressure weighing on my chest eases.

I trust my instincts. He won't do anything to hurt me.

"I'll tell you as we go up, but pay attention. You'll have to be a real actress."

Five minutes later, already on the floor where Cillian's offices are located, but still protected by the stairs, I stare at him with my mouth open.

"Why?"

"The man who hurt you. I think we know who he is, but to be sure, he'll need to expose himself. Do you understand what I'm saying? Can you do it?"

"What do you think? I'm half-Irish and I don't like people messing with what's mine."

Now he laughs openly.

"Focus on that. Keep that thought. It needs to be real."

"Does the woman who's part of this plan know?"

"No."

"So, how...?"

"He needed to *encourage her* today, let's say, but it's nothing she hasn't done before."

It takes me a few seconds to understand.

"Are you telling me it's something that happens regularly? That women go to his office to offer themselves?"

"She's one of our lawyers, not just any woman."

I swallow my anger, focusing on what I need to do.

"How did he know I was coming?"

"He knows everything."

"Not everything. Believe me when I say I won't need to rehearse to make a scene."

I head to his office, swinging the basket in my hand, completely forgetting about the *cupcakes*. They must have turned into a mess.

The worry about the sweets or feeding him, however, disappears when I enter the room and see the woman with her back to the door, topless, and if my guess is right, also without a bra.

"What the hell is going on here?"

There's not a hint of pretense in the amount of hate I'm feeling.

I want to kill her.

She looks back but doesn't seem shocked. Calmly, she picks up her shirt from the floor.

I'm shaking with rage, but she's no longer the target of my fury. The woman doesn't owe me any loyalty, but he does.

I walk in front of his desk, trying to focus on playing a role, but the pain tearing at my chest is real, as are the tears filling my eyes.

"Is this what you do at work?" I say, forcing myself to remember the lines Lorcan instructed me to say. "Are you betraying me?"

I don't look at him. I couldn't. The pain is too intense.

Suddenly, I feel naive.

Did I really think someone like him would choose me, with women like this at his disposal?

"To betray me, we'd need to have a commitment first. I don't recall asking you to come."

I can't stay here. Even though I know it's all part of the plan, my jealousy is real.

I'm suffocating.

"I'm not one of your whores anymore, *boss.*" I finish what I started, still recalling the words of his cousin. "It's over. You can keep her."

"Get her out of my sight," he tells Lorcan, and as his cousin puts his arms around my shoulders, I need to lean on him or risk falling, because my legs are weak.

When we reach the hallway, several people are leaving their offices. Some are members of the *Syndicate* who have even been to my bakery, but there are also older men.

I know I agreed to everything, but I'm dying of embarrassment. I feel exposed and humiliated.

"You did well," he tells me when we reach the stairs again.

I nod.

Yes, maybe I did well. The plan served to kill two birds with one stone. They'll manage to catch the man who tried to hurt me in the past, and on the other hand, I also rid myself of the illusion that I was enough for Cillian.

I DON'T SHED A TEAR. I'm used to crying inside and not showing weakness.

Rationally, everything that was done was for my benefit, I know, but then why do I feel so devastated?

Because you know that women like her must fall off a tree for him.

"We'll take you to your friend's house."

"What?"

"Elaine already knows we'll need her apartment."

"What do you mean?"

"The person who hurt you in the past needs to believe that you're vulnerable, Juno."

"No, I can't. She has a baby. I won't risk them getting hurt because of me."

"We know that, and she's safe, far from there. You have to agree with me that it's the perfect plan."

"If you suspect someone, why not just catch him?"

"There are three names. We're not sure who it is, but he knows he's being targeted and desperation will make him expose himself. You don't need to be afraid. He won't touch you. He just needs to think that you're weakened and that you've lost Cillian's protection after shouting at him in public. Anyone who knows my cousin knows he would never tolerate such disrespect."

I look at him, feeling exhausted.

"Tell me what I need to do. I just want this to be over."

Chapter 47

Cillian

I didn't readily agree with Lorcan's idea. It's not how I operate, based on subtleties.

I just wanted confirmation of who the son of a bitch was so I could avenge her and turn this page in our lives.

As a former agent, and maybe because I'm outside the situation, Lorcan was able to think more clearly.

Eventually, I said yes.

After today's meeting, we couldn't waste time because, intentionally, we only invited the three we suspected.

My cousin got in touch with *hackers* he has worked with before and in less than two hours, we had what we needed: we knew that of the three men who sat with us this afternoon, one was a pedophile.

I'm clenching my fist as I wait for the phone call that will lead me directly to the son of a bitch.

He would be my last resort and even now, I don't want to believe it's true. But Lorcan is sure it is.

I close my eyes and lean my head back on the chair in my office.

The pain on Juno's face when she saw the half-naked woman offering herself to me is something I won't be able to forget.

She knew it was all part of a plan, but I also know she saw beyond that. She understood that this isn't the first time it's happened.

Florence, the lawyer who unknowingly became part of the trap, was reassigned to the other coast. I would like to get rid of the woman once and for all, but even though she handles the legal side of my business, she still knows too much. The only options would be to send her to the other side of the country or kill her, and there was no reason for that.

My phone rings.

"There's someone going up to Elaine's apartment."

"Earlier than we expected."

"Yes. I'll get the information we need and then deal with him. Once I find out who the instigator is, I'll call you."

"Lorcan?"

"Yes?"

"Have Kellan take her to Orla's house. I don't want Juno to be alone."

"I don't think she's very inclined to follow your orders. She understood in a blink of an eye that Florence was once your lover."

"And Juno will be the mother of my children."

"What?"

"When this mess is over, I'm going to ask her to marry me."

"Not the best time for congratulations, huh?"

"No. Just keep my woman safe."

"And if she doesn't want to go to Orla's house?"

"She will go if I say so. Juno is not a coward. I'm what she wants. She won't turn her back without a fight."

I'M ON EDGE. I JUST need confirmation, but the anger controlling me is so intense that I've anticipated the next moves.

We're in a warehouse, about half an hour from Boston. The same three men who sat with me this afternoon are sweating as they try to maintain a feigned calm.

They act innocent, but I know that lying is almost a habit for them. It's part of their nature.

I'm staring at the one I'm almost sure is guilty. The same man who was like an uncle to me and who was under the protection of my blood family.

The monster who tried to abuse the girl who is now my wife.

"I thought we had already discussed everything that needed to be addressed in the meeting earlier," one of them finally speaks up.

"An unforeseen issue came up."

I don't look directly at my target. I like the idea of catching him by surprise. Even though he's suspicious of why he's been called here, he can't be sure.

"So, you and Grady's girl are together? She has a strong temper, judging by the shouting this morning," the one on my left says, smiling.

I weigh what I'm going to say because I know that the moment I do, one of the three men will have confirmation that he's going to die.

"Juno will be my wife."

I glance over them. They all show surprise, but it's not an unusual reaction.

"You didn't mention anything about this," Oisin says.

"I'm the boss. I don't need to account for my personal life to anyone."

From my peripheral vision, I see someone enter, but I don't divert my eyes from my guests.

"We need to talk," Kellan says.

"I'll be right back, gentlemen. I don't need to say that no one should leave here."

Even if they tried, there would be no way out, but it pleases me to know that the real culprit is sweating.

"What's going on?" I ask when we're outside.

"Everything is much more fucked up than you could imagine."

"What could be worse than having a pedophile among us? Than one of my trusted men being the same one who attacked my wife?"

"You have no idea. The guy who was digging into your target's life for Lorcan discovered something we never imagined."

He hands me a folder and as I start flipping through the pages, I say:

"I can't believe this shit."

"It's pretty crazy, right?"

"Or very convenient. A great excuse. Either way, it doesn't make a damn difference. He's going to die."

As if on cue, Lorcan arrives at the same time. He gets out of the car and opens the trunk. There's a man inside, and I know, without needing to ask, that he's the one who must have gone after Juno earlier today. Our bait.

My cousin pulls him out and removes the tape covering his mouth.

"Tell me who sent you," I command.

After I hear the name, I nod for Lorcan to take care of him.

I turn to my brother.

"The security around Juno must not be relaxed. Keep her with Orla until I'm done here. I won't be going home tonight."

Chapter 48

Juno

Hours Earlier

There was a man from Cillian inside Elaine's apartment when I arrived. Lorcan had explained it would be like this, but even knowing it was the plan, I felt terrible entering my friend's simple but well-kept house, knowing that someone would probably follow me to try to hurt me.

Bringing danger into Elaine and Jax's home seemed wrong.

They had thought of everything, down to the smallest details.

I left Cillian's building and spent some time pretending to wait for a cab. I made sure that anyone watching me would be convinced that I was on my own.

None of my bodyguards approached, but I knew I was being watched by them and that if they tried to attack me there, hell would break loose.

I look at the small living room and see some of Jax's toys scattered around. Lorcan told me that my friend and her son had been taken to Orla's house, which makes me feel more at ease.

My phone lights up with a message, and the single word makes the hair on the back of my neck stand on end.

"Prepare yourself."

My stomach is churning. I can hardly breathe. I know they won't let anyone out there hurt me, but fear isn't something you can rationalize.

232

I get up, feeling weak, and the man from Cillian gestures to me.

I know what I need to do, so I head to the small suite and enter the adjoining bathroom.

I turn on the shower and move to the shower stall, then pull the curtain. The man stays in the bedroom, probably hiding.

Minutes later, I hear the bathroom door open, and just like when the guy tried to take me from college, I can't help but tremble.

As in horror movies, the shower curtain is pulled aside.

Unlike Hollywood monsters, however, like the other guys from the *Syndicate*, his appearance is ordinary. Someone you'd bump into on the street without a second thought.

I see in his eyes that he realizes in a split second that something is wrong. I'm dressed.

I don't have time to do or say anything. Neither does he. In the next instant, Cillian's man appears and injects a syringe into his neck.

I don't move. My clothes are wet, as are my shoes, and I'm shivering from the cold.

Odhran enters the bathroom and turns off the shower. He picks me up and carries me out of the stall.

"I'm taking you to Orla's house. Orders from your man."

I don't argue. I just let myself be guided, and not even when the car stops in front of their aunt's house, minutes later, do I question.

Elaine and Orla come to greet me and hug me.

"Let's go inside, dear," Orla says. "You need to get out of these wet clothes."

"AFTER TODAY, YOU'LL finally be able to turn that page in your life, Juno."

"It wasn't that man who tried to hurt me in the past. He's too new."

Orla looks at me in silence before saying:

"How sensitive are you feeling? Do you want to hear the truth?"

"Yes, I do."

"According to what my nephew told me, the man who entered Elaine's apartment today has nothing to do with your past. He was sent just to silence you."

"So who is the real monster?"

"Someone trusted by Cillian. A man who will regret crossing your path one day."

"He's going to kill him," I say, certain of it.

"We shouldn't discuss this, Juno."

"I don't care if he dies."

My voice sounds apathetic. I'm exhausted.

"What's wrong, my daughter?"

I'm not sure if it's the tone she uses to ask or because I've held my emotions in for much longer than I thought I could, but it seems that the floodgates of my tears have opened.

"Juno, what happened?"

"Do you know about the setup this morning?"

"Vaguely."

"There was a woman with him. From what I understand, an ex-lover. She didn't even know it was all just a plan, yet she was there, almost naked, in front of Cillian, offering herself."

"My nephew wasn't a monk before you two got together."

"Yes, but knowing there were women in the past is one thing; seeing with my own eyes that these women have access to him at any time is another."

"My daughter, think about what you're saying."

"I don't understand."

"This 'having access,' as you said, doesn't work that way. I may not have been the best mother in the world to my nephews, but I taught them to be with one woman at a time. I'm not saying they're saints. They've all had their wild days and never committed, but I've never seen them with multiple women at the same time. Not even Odhran, who is the worst of them all."

"Why would he want to be with me when he can have anyone?"

"If you don't know the reason yet, maybe you're not ready for the answer. I know it's hard not to feel jealous of men like them. Look at me. I'm short, slim, and my face isn't exactly a beauty queen's. I'm ordinary. My husband was very similar in appearance to Kellan. Big and blonde. Powerful. He would draw attention wherever he went, even if he hadn't been who he was. At the beginning of our marriage, of course, I felt insecure. I'm human. I had self-esteem issues like any woman."

"And how did you deal with it?"

"With the attention from women, you mean?"

"Yes."

"My Eoin wasn't a romantic man, but until the day he left me, he never missed a chance to show me with actions and his body how loved I was. You're afraid of what it means to be Cillian's wife because of who he is, but marrying an ordinary guy wouldn't save you from being cheated on. If that were the case, all ugly men would be faithful."

For the first time since I found the woman in Cillian's room, I manage to smile.

"That's better," she says and hugs me. "If you want advice, don't anticipate too much. Trying to build a safety net, predict the future, won't help. Take a risk. Give him a vote of confidence. Love doesn't come with guarantees. You'll fight and hurt each other, but I can tell you that when the feeling is reciprocated, it's worth every second of any pain."

Chapter 49

Cillian

My breathing is ragged, but the hand holding the whip never rests.

Oisin's screams of pain or even the wide gashes on his back can't quell my rage.

He confessed everything, as I knew he would. Or rather, according to the report my brother gave me earlier, Aoife, his other personality, confessed.

I don't believe this shit, and even if I did, I wouldn't care. The body I'm punishing is that of the bastard who touched her. The voice and hands belong to the one who frightened Juno and triggered the tragedy that ended her father's life.

My fury doesn't diminish.

I've beaten him, tortured him, while making him detail his involvement in her life.

There are no more secrets between us at this moment. I know about the house he owns and had set aside to kidnap her and keep her subjugated and defenseless for years, maybe.

I know that every beating she endured, even with that bitch Doireann's consent, was an idea that came from him.

I know that most of the pain, tears, and fear my wife was subjected to originated in his sick mind.

He wanted the child, when he finally stole her, to understand that only he would love her. To accept him as a safe harbor after spending years suffering at the hands of her mother.

Perverted son of a bitch.

The whip is soaked in blood, but it's still not enough.

"I never really believed in hell," I say. "How could I, when to many, I am the devil himself? But now, I hope that there is an eternity and that you feel pain beyond death."

He lifts his head in his semi-conscious state.

"We're almost relatives."

"Who's speaking now, huh? Oisin? Aoife? It doesn't matter. The answer is the same for either of them: we are *nothing*."

The whip continues to crack through the air, but not even the smell of bloody flesh affects me.

"Mercy..."

"Don't waste your time. You're already dead."

I drop the whip and go to the tools to grab a scythe. In two quick strokes, I sever both hands. Those hateful hands that dared to touch her.

He passes out. It's not the first time today.

"Wake him up."

My men throw cold water on him, and he comes back to consciousness.

I approach with the gallon of gasoline and pour it entirely over his head.

He doesn't react anymore, and I almost want him to, but I know it's over.

I strike the match and watch for a long time as his body twists, hanging from the chains, and even when I'm sure he's gone, it doesn't seem enough.

I go to what's left of him — the two hands — rip off the ring, and put it in my pocket.

I finally feel ready to go meet her and free her from her past.

I ASKED THEM TO BRING her to my house.

With everything that happened, I know she's still hurt from the scene in my office and I don't want any witnesses to what we're going to discuss.

We've come to a crossroads, and now it's time to make choices. There's no more room for retreat.

I stayed under the shower for almost an hour, but I know that no matter how clean my flesh is, my soul can never be recovered.

I step out of the bathroom and am surprised to see her sitting on my bed.

I wasn't expecting that, but rather that I'd need to persuade her to come.

Shouts or perhaps some curses, but not just watching me as if trying to see inside me.

At first, she doesn't say anything, just staring back at me, but then she stands up and comes to where I am.

"I wanted to kill you. I don't like thinking about other women touching you. So many that I'll never know how many."

"It's the past."

"Don't break my heart, Cillian. Don't offer me heaven and then let me fall. I accept everything you are. I'll never judge you, but don't be disloyal to me."

"Being disloyal to you would mean being disloyal to myself, my wife. You are inside me, Juno. In every cell of mine."

"Show me."

"First, I need to tell you something."

"No. Later. Everything else can wait. Show me that I'm yours."

I watch her, trying to control the adrenaline coursing through me. Today, the monster has been awakened, and if I were a better person, I wouldn't even think of touching her. But I'm not. She knows this and accepts me anyway.

I drop the towel from my waist and she tries to lift the dress she's wearing.

"No. I'll do it."

I feel impatient, yet at the same time, I want it to last; the ravenous desire demands that I be the one to undress her. I won't be satisfied with anything less than her complete surrender.

"Turn around."

When she obeys, I unzip the dress, letting it fall to her feet. She removes her sandals on her own.

"Look at me, Juno."

Everything in my body aches for her. At this moment, I am more beast than human, because I want to mark her. To penetrate her body and forget for a moment that I am as much a monster as the one I killed today.

She seems to sense my need because she remains passive, usually so fiery.

Her submission ignites me, turning every piece of flesh in my body into uncontrollable, burning fire.

I kneel down, pull down her panties, and part the lips of her sex with my tongue.

She moans and grabs my hair.

"Later," I promise. "I have to enter you now."

I stand up and remove her bra, brushing the backs of my hands against her hardened nipples. I take one in my mouth, then the other, alternating between her sweetness.

I lift her into my arms and carry her to the bed.

I lie on my back and seat her on top of me.

My fingers touch her moisture, but she is too sensitive and needy. She doesn't want to wait.

"Too far. I can't tolerate any distance between us today," I say, sitting up.

I align our sexes and look at the place where our bodies are about to fit together.

The feminine softness of her body against my hardness.

The purity of her spirit against my filth.

Her innocence against the evil that resides in me.

Complements or opposites, it no longer matters. Juno is mine, and our lives are intertwined forever.

I lift her, almost making her kneel on the bed, and suck on her entire breast.

She whimpers with pleasure.

I don't touch her yet, except with my mouth. I slide my hands between us and part the lips of her pussy.

"You're going to feel every piece of me taking you."

She bites her lip as she begins to descend, her tight sex opening like a flower to accommodate my thickness.

Her eyes search mine, filled with passion.

"I love you," she says.

When I take her fully, she moans and closes her eyes, screaming my name.

I don't let her rise again, staying buried deep inside her body, my hands pulling her down by the shoulders.

"There's nothing I can say to you, be it love, passion, madness, that can explain what you are to me, Juno."

"I don't care. I'm yours. The title doesn't matter, words will never be stronger than the feeling."

We move together and I let her take control.

I lick her nipple and she grabs my neck tightly.

Juno pulses around my hardness.

Her legs close around my waist and she uses my shoulders to leverage her movements.

"Ahhhhhh..."

I almost pull out completely and when I thrust back in, the penetration isn't gentle; it's rough, urgent.

She tightens around me, almost making me come, her delicate pussy trying to accommodate my thick cock.

Kisses merge, thirsty, stealing our breath. Tongues devour each other, the rough rhythm of our fucking leaving us drenched in sweat.

The sensation of my cock inside and out of my wife's body engulfs me in a wave of lasciviousness.

I thrust deeply, making her descend forcefully, but it's not enough, so I position her on her hands and knees.

I pound relentlessly because I want to consume her, mix our scents and fluids. Never leave the sensual shelter of her sex.

I shift the angle of my hips and my hand travels to her clitoris. She arches against me, riding, even restrained under my control.

I increase the rhythm and she orgasms, squeezing me.

I grip the cheeks of her ass tightly and fill her completely, stretching her, pushing her to the limit between pleasure and pain.

It's a rough, passionate fuck.

The cadence of our bodies fills the silence of the night with lust.

"One more," I say, pinching her clitoris.

She throws her head back and when she surrenders again, it's my trigger. Crazy with desire, I spill inside her.

We don't move for a few seconds. I think we're both hesitant to undo this powerful and unique bond, this mixture of love and lust.

I pull out slowly because I know she's sensitive.

I lay her on her back and fit myself between her legs, our mouths almost touching.

"I don't have the right to ask you this, but I will anyway. Marry me. Be mine forever. Companion, mother of my children, queen."

"Promise me you'll honor our love and that you'll never betray me. Separate from me, but don't betray me."

"I won't betray you. I don't want anyone else. I'll never want anyone else. I have my everything, right here, in my arms."

Chapter 50

Cillian

Two Months Later

"The deal is over," I say more to my cousin than to anyone else. "With those fucked-up *Los Morales* practically off the map, I've done my part with Yerik."

"How long will they leave the six routes open?" Kellan asks.

"No deadline. They're ours for good," my cousin replies.

"Is your girl doing okay?" I ask, because even though I hate it, I know that Taisiya is his ward.

"As far as I know, yes. She doesn't call me all the time."

"She shouldn't ever call," I say.

He sighs, looking irritated. So do I.

"Should we get back to this?"

"No. Unless you're planning to marry a Russian, I don't see a problem with checking on her from time to time."

"Is she pretty? She has to be, right? That's the only thing that justifies all this concern," Odhran mocks, and Lorcan scowls.

"She's studying to be a nun, damn it."

"That's not what I asked. Or are only the ugly ones brides of Jesus? As far as I know, her sister, Maxim's wife, also spent years in a convent and now she's married."

"Fuck, you guys are hell-bent on annoying me. Yes, she's fucking gorgeous. A true goddess, but also broken, even if she doesn't

244

remember everything she's been through. Even if Taisiya didn't follow the religious path, I'm the last person she should be involved with."

"Enough, kids," Kellan says, struggling not to laugh. "Let's leave Lorcan to his divine contest for his girl's love."

"I'm leaving," my cousin says, standing up. "I'm going to Juno's bakery to pick up a box of *cupcakes* she made especially for me."

"I'm coming too," Odhran announces.

"My wife sent a message," I tell my younger brother. "She said that if you hurt Elaine, she'll personally cut off your balls."

"I have no idea what you're talking about," he deflects, "I'm just going for sugar. Even though the brunette is a treat, only bile comes out of that mouth."

"I DON'T WANT TO SCARE you," she says, lying on my chest after we've fucked for hours.

"I don't scare easily, *baby*."

"Unless it concerns me, right?"

"What's wrong?" I ask, making her straddle my body.

"It might not be anything major, but you haven't mentioned Joe Pineda again."

"Because he's probably no longer here. There isn't a stone in this country we haven't turned over. The son of a bitch has disappeared."

"Why do I feel like you're not telling me everything?"

"Because I never tell everything. You don't need to know the filth of my world."

She lowers her head.

"It's mine too, in a way."

"Are you regretting it?"

"Never. I love you. It's with you I want to spend the rest of my days."

I sit up so we can look at each other.

"What I keep hidden is to protect you."

"I know, but I need to know at least the basics."

"Like what?"

"Who our enemies are."

"No, but I can tell you that the issue with the Salvadorans will be closed soon. I was just waiting for your graduation. I let them think that with Joe out of the way..."

"He *is* out of the way?"

"If he's not, we'll find him soon. Anyway, I let them think that with the son of a bitch out of the way, I had forgotten what they did to you."

"But you haven't forgotten?"

"No. I don't care who was responsible. They breached the college and tried to take you. There's no forgiveness for that. If their leader can't control his own men, he's unfit to lead. Now, tell me what's still bothering you."

"Elaine thinks someone was watching us from outside the store. She went very pale."

"When?"

"This week. She even showed me, but said that when the person realized we were looking back, they disappeared. What should we do?"

"Nothing. I'll take care of it."

She stays silent, and I know something still worries her.

"What are you thinking?"

"I don't want to put my clients at risk. If it's Joe lurking around... could he come in and do something crazy?"

"No, but as I said, I'll take care of it."

"And the rest of their organization members? Won't they seek retaliation?"

"How could they? Dead men don't fight."

Chapter 51

Juno

Weeks Later

Cillian killed the monster from my childhood. The man who tormented me and made me have nightmares even as an adult.

He didn't tell me outright that he did it, but I know that's what happened because that same night he proposed to me, and after making love with me twice more, he gave me a ring just like the one he wears.

Inside, it was engraved with *Oisin O'Sullivan*, which means my monster now has a name and surname.

A few days ago, I did an online search, and he's listed as "missing," but not as a criminal. Instead, he's a financial sector businessman who hasn't been seen for weeks.

He has a wife, children, and grandchildren, and I felt nauseous looking at his smiling face posing with his family.

Do they have any idea that the bastard was a child abuser? Would they believe he was complicit with a cruel mother who used her own daughter as a punching bag?

If I hadn't woken up that day, God only knows what could have happened to me.

"Juno Cavanagh" the announcer calls me, and I climb the stairs to receive my diploma, my legs shaky.

While I'm up there on stage, I don't bother looking for the owner of my heart among the crowd. I know he's not there but waiting for me inside the car.

It's these details that make me understand we're not a typical couple. We will never stroll down the street holding hands for ice cream in the middle of summer, because enemies are everywhere.

In the audience, my aunt Eimear, whose trip from Ireland was courtesy of Cillian, who thought she should be present at this important moment in my life, smiles along with Orla, Elaine, and the handsome Jax.

I wave to them and laugh when I see my friend put two fingers to her lips and whistle.

After shaking the professor's hand, I receive my diploma and pose for photos. Then, I run to join the four of them.

"Official sweet-maker now," I say, waving the fake diploma, since the real one will only be ready in a few days.

Everyone is smiling, but when I focus on Elaine's face, I see her brow furrow.

"What's wrong?"

"I... I think I saw someone. It must have been my imagination."

My aunt is holding Jax, so after accepting kisses from her and Orla, I pull my friend aside.

"What happened? You're pale again, like that day at the bakery when you said we were being watched."

"I think I saw someone from my past."

"An ex? Jax's father?"

She looks like she's about to faint.

"No. Nothing like that."

"Girl, you're really scaring me. Do you want me to talk to Cillian?"

"No. Not for now."

"Okay, but let's make a deal: if this ghost shows up again, you have to promise me you'll let me know. Promise me."

"You have my word. I'll tell you."

I keep watching her for a while longer, trying to see if she changes her mind, but she leaves me alone and goes back to her son.

Half an Hour Later

"CONGRATULATIONS ON your graduation, *baby*."

"Oh my God, so many gifts!"

Despite what I say, I'm not interested in what appear to be jewelry boxes, but in jumping into his lap. That's exactly what I do.

"Don't you want to see your surprises?"

"No. I miss this mouth of yours."

"Which part of you?" he whispers in my ear, sending shivers down my spine.

"All of me, my love."

He holds my neck and gives me a wet kiss.

"Add sucking your pussy all night as another present."

"Seriously? I thought that was a constitutional right of mine."

I get a smack on the ass in response.

"Open the smaller box. I hadn't bought your engagement ring yet."

I do as he says and am left speechless when I see a ring with a huge teardrop-shaped diamond.

"Cillian, it's beautiful!"

"Now we're officially engaged."

"I don't need a piece of jewelry to know that."

He looks at me seriously.

"There's something I need to tell you."

"About what?"

"Joe Pineda. He's no longer a problem. Consider it a present as well."

Cillian doesn't need to be more explicit for me to understand what he's saying: the Salvadoran is dead.

Despite that, he doesn't seem at ease, and I frown, confused.

"Isn't that good news?"

"Partially. His uncle, the leader of the *M de Muerte*, is missing."

"I thought the problem was the nephew."

"Not just him," he says, without elaborating further.

"Am I at risk?"

"Aside from the fact that you're my wife?"

"That's a known risk; I'm talking about hidden ones."

"As much as I am. Organizations don't go to war against people but against other organizations."

"Should I be worried?"

"No. I'll handle it for both of us. Live, my beautiful wife, and let me slay the dragons."

"I'm not a fragile doll."

"No, you're not, but you don't need to prove it to anyone. Just to me."

Chapter 52

Cillian

Caribbean

Cillian and Juno's Wedding Day

Three Months Later

I discreetly pull at the collar of my shirt, trying not to show the men in my family how nervous I am as I wait for my wife to walk down the aisle set up on the beach and tell the world that we belong to each other.

The place we chose for the definitive *I do* is a Caribbean island I recently bought.

Lorcan mentioned to me that Russians owned islands, and I wondered why the hell I hadn't thought of that myself.

It's the perfect place to find peace—a rare commodity in my life—with my wife, and in the near future, I hope, to bring our children here.

I look toward the end of the runway and can't see if she has arrived yet.

Whose idea was it to set up some sort of covered walkway? Besides the fact that it must be hellishly hot in there, I can't see her approaching.

I know my aunt and hers—who came from Ireland with the cousins specially for our wedding—are by her side, and also that the island is safe.

This time, my anxiety isn't about my obsessive concern for Juno but because I don't want to wait any longer to make her mine.

"Jesus, man, calm down," Lorcan says.

"I don't know what you're talking about," I deflect.

The little boy, Elaine's son, comes running down the red carpet and trips. In a split second, my younger brother reaches him and picks him up. Despite seeming to dislike each other, Jax, the boy, is a sort of link between Odhran and Juno's employee, now manager.

The music starts and damn, I finally get to see her.

I smile when I see that she doesn't seem nervous at all but radiant.

I don't pay attention to her dress or the way her hair is styled.

It's Juno's smile that captivates me. Her happiness is mine too. The shadows that used to always be present in her eyes are dissolving more and more each day.

She still has her moments of introspection, and I know it's when she remembers the past. I don't have the power to erase that, but I can build a new path for both of us.

She walks down the aisle smiling, her sensual hips swaying unconsciously, and as always, leaving me mesmerized.

She didn't want to walk down the aisle with my brothers and told me she hopes her father, wherever he is, can see that she has never replaced him.

I descend the two steps to meet her and, unable to wait for the order we were told to follow, I pull her into my arms.

"I thought you didn't like public displays of affection," she says.

"I don't, but I could never resist you. I never will."

Honeymoon

Days Later

"YOU KICKED OUT OUR relatives," she says, laughing.

"They didn't take the hint, so I had to do it my way."

"And in this case, 'doing it your way' means announcing in the middle of dinner that we needed privacy to make babies? Jesus!"

"I've never been accused of being a diplomat, woman."

"Well, I can't deny that."

We're lying on loungers near the water. Juno is wearing nothing but a tiny bikini bottom. She's topless, as she has been every day, and her nipples, once light pink from the sun, are now a darker shade.

She says something, but I have no idea what it is.

"I can't focus on conversations with you parading those beautiful tits in front of me. I want to have you ride me and suck them, no matter who's watching."

"There's no one else, remember? You sent all the men away so I could..." she makes air quotes with both hands "parade my beautiful tits in front of you."

Without waiting for a response, she climbs onto my body, her full breasts almost brushing against my mouth.

"You sent everyone away to make babies, but you're late, husband."

I hold her face, the desire to play vanishing completely.

She smiles, but she also looks serious now as she takes my hand and places it on her belly.

"We already have a little one on the way, Cillian."

"Are you serious?"

"Yes, I am. I stopped taking the pill. I wanted to surprise you."

"But what about the plans to expand the bakery? The factory for events?"

It was no secret that I wanted children immediately. I'm open to the number, actually, but for the sake of Juno's youth and also because her business is doing very well, I didn't pressure her when we talked about it.

She reclines and lies on my body.

"I don't want to wait. Life is short. Mothers all over the world work and take care of their families. I'll manage."

"I have no doubt about that."

"So, are you happy?"

"More than happy, woman. A family will be the crowning glory of our love."

She falls silent, and I lift her chin so she will look at me. I think I know what she's thinking.

"I'll protect them with my life. Don't be afraid."

"And yourself too? Because I don't want to live without you like Orla lived without her husband."

"I can't promise to live forever or even to a certain age, but I can swear that every breath I take on this Earth will be for you and our children. You are my air, Juno."

Epilogue 1

Juno

Boston

Day of Luke's Birth

Months Later

When I married Cillian, I thought it was the happiest day of my life, and it was, but the feeling of having my child in my arms, nursing, receiving his nourishment from my body, is unparalleled.

I watch the beautiful, healthy little boy, a piece of both of us, feeling my eyes fill with tears.

"Thank you," I say, lifting my face to look at my husband.

Our family is outside the room because I asked to have this moment with just my two men.

"I don't know what to say. I never know what to say." He moves closer, takes my hand, and places it over his chest, at heart level. "With you, I only know how to feel."

The organ he once vowed never to have is beating rapidly, and I can see from his face that he feels emotional, but Cillian, like me, was not taught to show or understand his own emotions.

"I told you once. I don't need words. I have you adoring me every moment. We have a home and now, a child. No ready phrase will ever translate what you two are to me. What we are to each other."

Months Later

"HEY, DAD, IT'S ME AGAIN. I hope you've been well since the last time we met. I had the grass around your grave changed because I like to see that you're being cared for."

I run my hand over the new gravestone that Cillian had made with the phrase I chose: *Eternal longing from the luckiest daughter in the world for having you as a father.*

I wipe away a tear that falls on my cheek.

"Every month it's the same thing, right? I promise not to cry, but I end up doing just that. I'm sorry for being so emotional. Lately, I haven't been able to control myself. Actually, I was like this the entire pregnancy, but since your grandson was born, everything brings me to tears. Cillian says he's not good with words. I'm worse, but I'll never stop trying to tell you how much I love and miss you, Dad. I hope one day I can forgive myself for telling you what Doireann did to me. For now, I still can't. Cillian's aunt says I need therapy because it will be very difficult to align my mind on my own. Maybe she's right, but I don't think I'm ready yet. Well, I have to go. It's almost time for Luke's feeding, and the boy is a real little calf."

I stand up and am surprised to see my husband waiting for me.

He walks over to where I am and pulls me into an embrace.

"I thought you were away."

"I came back early."

I smile.

"And how did you find me here?"

"I *knew* you were here. Haven't you figured out that I'm your stalker? The most obsessed one?"

"Do I have others?"

"No. I made sure of that," he says, no longer joking.

I don't want to bring a heavy mood between us, which always happens when we talk about my and Luke's safety.

"Stalk me, husband. I don't mind. Being by your side isn't a prison; it was a choice. There's no freedom away from you."

Epilogue 2

Cillian

Caribbean

Five Years Later

"And the *monster* died. Yay..." My little girl, Ciara, cheers as she claps her hands when I finish telling her one of her favorite stories.

I kiss her on the head, and then she runs off to find her brother.

"She loves that story," Juno says, sitting on my lap and wrapping her arms around my neck.

"She does. Especially the part where the monster is defeated. One day, she'll know that the monster is her father."

Juno kisses me slowly, as she does when she wants to tell me something without words. When she vows her love and fidelity in silence.

"She'll love you the same way, just as I loved my father."

"But what if she could choose?"

"I wouldn't trade him for anyone else. He adored me with all his heart. For a long time, I thought he killed himself out of love for Doireann."

"He didn't. He was asking for a divorce."

"What? You never told me that!"

"I must have forgotten. I found out, after you returned to Boston, that Grady was filing for divorce and also requesting full custody of you. The process didn't go through because Doireann slept with the lawyer."

I don't go into detail about how I had him killed in prison because it wouldn't add anything to her story.

"For a long time, I thought Dad loved her more than me. That's why he left me, but even before you told me about the divorce, I had already concluded that he didn't. He killed himself thinking he failed me. Out of guilt, which is a feeling I understand well."

"Before I brought you into my life, as an adult, I mean, I never had remorse."

"And you started feeling it because of me? Because you wanted a different life for yourself?"

"No, Juno. Everything that exists in me is yours and our children's. I love you with every breath, and I will love you after I die, I'm sure of it, but the remorse I feel about you and our children isn't because I wish I had done something differently, but because I know that, even if given the choice, I would do everything the same."

"Because the *Syndicate* is part of who you are."

"Yes. Because the *Syndicate* is part of who I am. I can't imagine myself in another life. I was raised to lead my Organization. I'm cruel to my enemies because I don't understand the concept of forgiveness or love except in relation to our family. I'm indifferent to most human beings."

"But you love us above all."

"Above all. Every beat of my merciless heart is for you."

"I never dreamed of a prince, Cillian. I never even dreamed of love. I don't care how others label us. I love you and I know I am loved. I see the adoration and care you have for our children. We may not be the family the world calls perfect, but we are a family and we have love in abundance."

The End!

Did you love *Dragon's Vow*? Then you should read *Forbidden Flames* by Amara Holt!

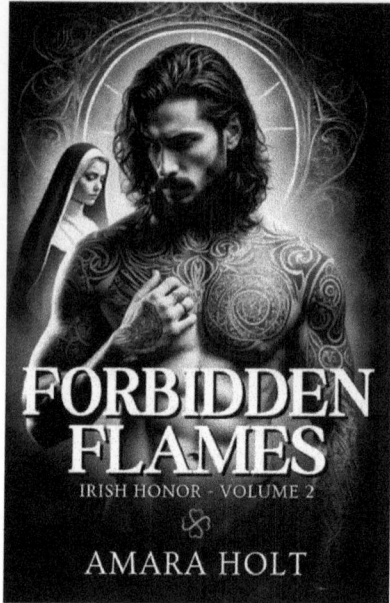

Forbidden Flames

In the world of crime, **love** is the ultimate danger.

Lorcan, known as "**The Irish Bomb**," is the ruthless right-hand man of the Irish Syndicate, feared for his **volatile temper** and **brutal tactics**. When his grandfather, the legendary ex-Pakhan Ruslan, tasks him with finding a missing Russian mafia princess, Lorcan expects just another mission. But the **fiery bond** that ignites between him and the innocent Taisiya is anything but ordinary.

Taisiya, a young woman who once dreamed of becoming a nun, finds her world **shattered** after a harrowing ordeal. Rescued by Lorcan, she struggles to piece together her lost memories, finding **solace** only in the arms of her **dangerous savior**. Their connection is undeniable, but with two powerful mafia families ready to tear them apart, their love could spark a **war** that no one can control.

Forbidden Flames is a gripping tale of **forbidden love**, fierce loyalty, and **unstoppable passion**. Dive into this dark and seductive romance where every **kiss** could be their last, and every **secret** could be their undoing.

Perfect for fans of **mafia romance, enemies-to-lovers**, and **intense**, heart-pounding drama, **Forbidden Flames** will leave you **breathless** and **begging for more**.

About the Author

Amara Holt is a storyteller whose novels immerse readers in a whirlwind of suspense, action, romance and adventure. With a keen eye for detail and a talent for crafting intricate plots, Amara captivates her audience with every twist and turn. Her compelling characters and atmospheric settings transport readers to thrilling worlds where danger lurks around every corner.